Bad to the Scone

Copyright © 2025 by London Lovett

All rights reserved.

No part of this book may be reproduced in any form or by any electronic or mechanical means, including information storage and retrieval systems, without written permission from the author, except for the use of brief quotations in a book review.

ISBN: 9798319481269

Imprint: Independently published

BAD to the SCONE

LONDON LOVETT

one
. . .

THE EVENING MOUNTAIN sky was flecked with silver stars, and it looked so vast you could easily believe that the universe went on forever. The spring night was laced with whispers of fresh pine and perfumy lilac and earthy moss ... and the familiar, much-loved scent of Cade's soap. It was earthy and comforting, at least to me, because it always surrounded me whenever I was wrapped in his arms. We'd dragged a blanket, some wine and a board loaded with cheese, crackers, nuts and grapes out to his back deck for a picnic under the stars. After nibbling cheese and sipping wine, I'd settled myself between his legs, so I could use him as both a backrest and a coat. His big arms held me in place, providing me with shelter from the air that had dropped precipitously in temperature once the sun had signed off for the night.

I twisted my face and peered up at him. He had a pensive, contemplative look on his face as he stared up at the night sky.

"What's on your mind, Mr. Rafferty? You look very deep in

thought. Contemplating the meaning of your existence in this universe?"

Cade chuckled and tightened his arms around me, and I snuggled closer to his comforting warmth. "Nothing quite so philosophical, I'm afraid. I was thinking about that old song by Jim Croce, the one about 'time in a bottle.' Every once in a while, I land myself in a perfectly amazing situation, like now, with you here in my arms under this incredible sky, and I always have the same thought. How do I capture this moment in a bottle? That way I could put it on a shelf, and when I'm feeling irritated or sad, I could take the bottle down, open it and revisit this moment."

"See, that was far more philosophical than you give yourself credit for. It was also a little Roald Dahl-ish. His character Big Friendly Giant keeps dreams in a jar, then he blows them into the rooms of sleeping children." I took his hands and snugged his arms even tighter around me like I might do with the ends of a shawl. "But your plan is much more romantic." A breeze ruffled the surrounding trees. Even wrapped in his warmth, I shivered. The calendar said it was spring, but it always came a little slower to the higher elevations. Stubborn patches of snow were still piled between tufts of new, green grass and wildflowers in Cade's garden. Cade had inherited a vast estate with tons of land and a mansion built a century before by his great grandfather, Arthur Gramby. By the time the property landed in Cade's hands, Arthur's dream home had lost most of its grandeur and sheen … as well as many windows and shingles. Cade was slowly bringing the home and surrounding gardens back to their former glory.

"I'm thinking we should move this picnic inside," Cade said. "It's getting cold, and I have something—I bought you something," he said, almost shyly, and if there was one thing Cade Rafferty lacked, it was shyness.

I reluctantly left his arms, and we worked together to gather up our picnic supplies. My mind poked around trying to guess what he'd bought me. I was like a kid shaking gifts under the tree (but more sophisticated). We rarely bought each other things, mostly because neither of us needed much. I'd never been the type who needed to be showered with flowers and candy (although candy I never turned down) and Cade liked the simple life. He bought the occasional nice sweater and new pair of hiking boots, but most of his money went into restoring the house.

I carried the cheese tray and wine inside, and Cade went through to his sitting room to spread out the blanket. The massive stone fireplace was dark tonight, but during the winter months, when snow fell from the sky, we always settled in front of a roaring fire with our mugs of cocoa. The room was lined with tall windows that looked out over the back of the property. Cade's restoration project had focused on the front tiered gardens, the ones leading up to the house from the road, but the back of the property was wild and overgrown and dotted with spruce, pine and ash trees. Cade had decided to leave it like that, natural, so elk, deer and even moose frequently wandered through the property. The big windows provided the perfect lookout, so he could watch the animals in their natural habitat without human interference.

I settled myself back down on the blanket. Cade still had an unusually coy look on his face. "Be right back." He left the room.

And then it hit me—a ring? Was Cade planning to propose? For a second, a thrill went through me, then a whole slew of emotions tangled up into a ball in my chest. Did I want a ring? I loved Cade. There was no question of that, but before I moved back to Ripple Creek, I'd been in a long-term relationship and engagement with Jonathan Rathbone. I'd convinced myself that the apprehension I felt about marrying Jonathan had been wedding jitters, but it took a few big events, like Nana going missing, a murder in town and my childhood crush returning to Ripple Creek, to stir up old feelings and bring me to the brilliant conclusion that I was marrying the wrong man. I'd had no such apprehension with Cade—ever—but leaving Jonathan and becoming an independent woman had allowed me to finally open my dream bakery. I loved my life right now, my business, my wonderful hometown, being back with my beloved grandmother and, of course, my incredibly perfect boyfriend. Would an engagement mess this perfection up? I hated that I wasn't entirely sure I wanted a proposal, and at the same time, I didn't want to lose Cade.

I'd worked myself into quite a mental lather by the time Cade returned, obviously hiding something behind his back. He wore a serious expression, but there was also a hint of a smile, a sweet smile like a young boy about to present a bouquet of freshly picked field daisies to his crush.

"I know we aren't big on giving each other gifts, but I got the advance for my new book last week, and I couldn't resist." He pulled a long velvet box out from behind his back. It was jewelry but not a ring. I was slightly disheartened at how relieved I felt knowing he wasn't about to propose. I was blaming it all on the terrible Rathbones. The breakup and cancellation of an elaborate wedding (the ridiculously expensive wedding I never wanted) had left me scarred and horrified about marriage.

Cade sat on the blanket and tried to tone down his beaming

smile. He was always urbane and understated, and that was what I loved about him. "I will warn you, I'm not well-versed on jewelry selection. I had a traumatic experience as a kid."

I laughed. "A traumatic jewelry shopping experience?" I asked. The velvet box sat unopened on the blanket between us.

"I spent all my allowance on this big, colorful beaded necklace for my mom. It had red and yellow and green baubles, and the more I think about it, the more I realize how ugly it was, but, at the time, I really thought it was something grand. I was sure my mom would gush about it and wear it wherever she went, grocery shopping, lunch with her friends, holiday parties. Let's just say her reaction was one of muted amusement. And no, she did not wear it out of the house … ever. And so now you know the sad story of my first jewelry buying experience."

I picked up the green velvet box. "Well, it doesn't look big enough for gaudy baubles, so maybe you've improved." I opened the box. A thin, glittering gold chain was dotted with small, opalescent pearls. It was gorgeous. "Oh, Cade," I said, my throat tightening. Seconds earlier, I worried he was going to propose, and now I was staring at a beautiful gift that already meant a great deal to me, and I hadn't even lifted it out of the box.

I picked up the delicate chain and turned around on my bottom so Cade could put it on. I lifted my hair, and a tremble of delight went through me as his warm breath tickled the back of my bare neck. His fingers grazed my skin as he closed the clasp. I patted the necklace. It was short, almost choker length. "I need to look in a mirror." I got up and walked into the powder room off the entry. The necklace was just what I would have picked for myself. Cade knew me too well.

I returned to the sitting room. Cade was leaned back on his

hands with his long legs stretched out in front of him. The low lights in the room highlighted his extraordinary features and hazel eyes. "Well? Do you think you might wear it out of the house? If not, then I'll understand."

I walked over and knelt next to him on the blanket. "It's perfect. It's a hundred-percent Scottie Ramone." I leaned over and kissed him.

"Oh, I almost forgot the bonus that came with the necklace." He left the room and returned seconds later with a plastic clamshell box filled with chocolate covered strawberries. "The jewelry store was giving them out with a purchase."

"Yum, well done, jewelry store." We spent the next few minutes eating chocolate covered strawberries. "You're right. We need one of those time-catching bottles. This night is a keeper."

Cade nodded as he took a bite of strawberry. A chunk of chocolate fell on his shirt. I snatched it and ate it before he could get it. I shrugged. "Finders, keepers." I touched the necklace again. "Thank you, Cade. I really love it."

"Figured it was time for nice jewelry." His gaze landed softly on me. "I'm glad the way things turned out between us, Scottie."

"I am, too." Our friendship had teetered on the edge of something more for months, but I'd been trapped in a muddle about my feelings for Dalton Braddock, the boy I'd always loved growing up. After some time and reflection, I realized that while I'd always have feelings for Dalton, they weren't the same intense, edge-of-heartbreak kind that I'd had growing up. And then Cade walked into my life, and he was nothing short of spectacular. We'd formed an almost instant bond, and after a rift, which ended with him leaving for a long book tour, I realized he was the one I wanted. Now he'd moved things to a new level with the necklace, which spurred a new thought in my mind. It was time to reveal my secret. It wasn't a secret that would harm our relationship, but it was one significant enough that I didn't want to keep it from him anymore.

"Cade, I need to tell you something." I hadn't said it with an ominous tone, but he took it that way.

"You've been secretly married to Braddock all this time," he said half-jokingly and half-not jokingly. To say that Cade and Dalton were enemies was an understatement.

I raised my brows in shock. "Seriously?"

"Sorry. Old scars and all that." Cade had suffered no small amount of hurt and dismay about my erratic feelings for Dalton.

I wasn't sure if I wanted to continue. His suggestion had upset me.

Cade reached for my hand. "I'm sorry. I don't know why I said that. I guess the evening was just going too well, so I needed to put an end to that. It's something I'm well-known for."

I tugged his hand. "Stop. I'm rich. That's what I wanted to tell you."

His misstep had ruined my entire speech.

Cade blinked at me, confused. "As in rich with life experiences?"

I shook my head. "Nope. The other kind of rich. The one where the bank sends me free calendars and pens almost constantly." I sighed. "Jeez, this went so much smoother in my head. You know that my parents died when I was young, and I was their only child, so I inherited everything. Well, they had a lot of money. They were, by every measure, extremely wealthy. Aside from their personal successes, my dad came from money, big money, old money. Then his mother, Grandmother Katherine died. My dad was *her* only child and—"

"You were his only child, so the whole pot of gold came to you," Cade finished for me.

"Right." I waited for more of a response but didn't get one. "Are you all right?" I asked because clearly this whole thing hadn't landed well.

"Why the secret? Why didn't you think you could tell me?"

"Honestly, because my money just never came up. I don't think about it much. I have everything I need regardless of my bank account."

"Was it a trust issue?" he asked.

"What? No, of course not." My phone beeped with a text. I never ignored my phone in case Nana needed me. I glanced at it. It was a text from Nana. "I ned U." Nana wasn't a great texter, but this was odd even for her. I showed it to Cade. "What do you think this means?"

"I ned U," he read, then his eyes rounded. "I need you."

My heart rate sped up, and I called Nana. She answered. I knew instantly something was wrong. Her voice was weak and thready. "Button, I fell."

"I'm on my way." I hung up and turned to Cade. "Nana fell. I've got to go."

"Do you want me to come?" His tone was dry. He was still processing my secret, the secret that for some reason had put him on defense. It was a spectacularly bad ending to an otherwise spectacular night.

"No, I'll be fine." I grabbed my purse and hurried out the door without saying goodbye.

two
. . .

I WAS in full adrenaline rush mode by the time I reached Nana's cottage. There was only one light on inside. I flew out of the car, raced up the steps and opened the door. Nana was in our small front room sitting on the couch and holding a bag of frozen vegetables on her arm. The edge of the area rug was flipped over like a dog ear.

I reached her and sat gently on the couch. "Was it the rug?" I motioned toward the turned-up corner.

"Yes, I need to tape those darn corners down."

I looked at the bag of frozen peas. "Do you think it's broken?"

She lifted the bag slowly. Her wrist was red from the ice, and the small curve on the arm assured me it was broken. "It doesn't look too bad," she said.

"We've got to go to the hospital, Nana. It needs to be x-rayed. It looks broken."

Nana winced from the pain as she placed the icy bag back on her wrist. For the first time in my life, my intelligent, confident and fiercely independent grandmother looked fragile and vulnerable. Nana had taken me in without question after my parents' deaths. My mom had made sure that if anything happened to them, her mom, Nana, would become my guardian. I was so thankful to my mom for that decision. Grandmother Katherine was a nice, respectable woman, but I would have been terribly unhappy in her high-society lifestyle. Nana had been the opposite of Katherine in every way, and as horrible as it was to be without a mom and dad, I never lacked for anything emotionally or physically growing up in Nana's humble little mountain cottage.

"Can you get my shawl, Button? It got chilly this evening."

Cade texted as I parked in the hospital lot. "How is Nana?"

"Broken wrist, I think. We're heading into the hospital right now."

"Let me know if there's anything I can do. And I'm sorry tonight ended badly."

"Me, too. We'll talk tomorrow."

I got out and walked around to the passenger side. Nana was already climbing out on her own. I placed a hand under the elbow of her good arm. "Don't fuss, Scottie. I'm fine." If there was one thing my grandmother hated it was to be coddled and treated like she was old and feeble.

"Says the woman with a bag of frozen peas on her arm. Nana, remember when I fell out of Deedee Rhode's tree and broke my arm? You wouldn't let me do anything on my own even though it was just a tiny break. It's my turn to return the favor—"

Nana laughed. That was my grandmother. She found humor in everything. "There are two ways to interpret that promise. One is filled with pureness and one has a touch of revenge. I remember trying to help you wash your hair in the shower, and you were so angry you threw the soap at me."

"I was just old enough to consider anyone, even my grandmother, seeing me naked as the highest form of indignity."

We reached the hospital entrance, and the big doors slid open. An attendant was passing the entrance. She looked at us. "Does she need a wheelchair?" she asked politely.

Nana looked pointedly down at her feet. "They're both still working just fine, thank you very much."

The attendant looked taken aback. "We're fine. Thank you for asking," I said with a weak smile.

"Nana, let's get you checked in."

"Oh, look, it's Dalton," she said with a bright smile. Dalton was wearing his ranger uniform. He was walking down the hall from the ambulance entrance. Even though Dalton and I never ended up together, Nana still adored him. She often invited him to lunch or dinner, mostly when I was out, thank goodness. "Dalton, why are you here?" Nana asked airily, her injury apparently all but forgotten. "You're not hurt, are you?"

Dalton's brow wrinkled in concern. "There was an accident on the highway, but what's happened? Did you hurt your arm?"

Nana scoffed. "I think Scottie is overreacting. Just a little sprain."

Dalton looked at me, and I shook my head to let him know it was not a sprain.

"I'm sorry to hear about this, Evie. Let me know if there's anything I can do." His gaze fleetingly landed my direction, then he returned his focus to Nana. "I'll stop by the house tomorrow to check on you."

Nana reached up with her good hand and patted the side of his face. "Such a gentleman. Thank you, Dalton."

"Nana, we need to get you checked in," I reminded her. Dalton and I exchanged our usual polite smiles. We'd been great friends at one time, but my relationship with Cade had put a freeze on that friendship. We were congenial and spoke in casual terms still, but that was the extent of it.

Dalton left and I walked Nana to the check-in desk. I pulled my phone out while we waited. It was late, but I was sure my bakery assistant, Jack, would see my message in the morning before he left for work. "I might be late to work. My grandmother broke her wrist, and we're waiting to get it taken care of. I'll get there as soon as I can." I pushed the phone into my pocket.

The one drawback of owning a bakery was the early start to the workday. Most of the time I didn't mind it. I was in a routine, so it was easy to get up before dawn. I liked how quiet and deserted the town was when I arrived at work. It was a peaceful way to start a hectic day at the shop. But on rare occasions, like tonight, I knew I wouldn't be in bed at a good hour. That meant my alarm was going to wake me from a dead sleep, and the rest of my day would follow suit.

Nana finished answering the questions and turned to me. Her face was pale, and she had dark rings under her eyes. This had shocked her more than she was letting on. I took her arm, and this time she didn't complain.

"Oh, Button," she said with an exhausted sigh. "That darn rug."

"I know, Nana, but this won't be bad. They'll set the arm, and

I'll tell Hannah to come sit with you tomorrow until I get home from work."

We sat in two of the green vinyl chairs. There were a few people with masks and obvious coughs a couple seats down. The last thing Nana needed was to leave the hospital with an illness. "Let's move down a few more places, Nana." She understood the reasoning behind my suggestion.

Nana settled into her chair, and that was when she noticed my new jewelry. "Button, what a pretty necklace." Her eyes sparkled for the first time all evening. My grandmother could produce an eye sparkle like no other. "Is it from Cade?"

I touched it gently. "Yes, he gave it to me tonight."

The sparkle faded. "And I ruined your night with my silly accident."

I shook my head. "No, actually, I ruined it all on my own."

Nana looked puzzled. "What do you mean?"

"I'll tell you later. Right now, let's just focus on getting you back to your perfectly spry self."

three

...

I DRIZZLED THE WHITE, sugary glaze in stripes over the freshly baked strawberry scones. I stared down at the tray through bleary eyes. I'd been in a drowsy haze all morning. Nana and I had gotten home from the hospital just before midnight. The fracture was small, and she wouldn't require surgery, which was a huge relief. The doctor also said her vitals and bloodwork were amazing for someone her age. While her friends were always complaining about maladies and making constant trips to the doctor, Nana rarely had health issues, and she just as rarely visited a doctor. It was such a relief to hear how fit she was; Nana and I hugged for a long time. It occurred to me then that Nana had wanted to skip the trip to the hospital because she worried she'd hear bad news from the attending physician, news that would have nothing to do with a broken wrist. Growing up, I always fretted over losing her. She was obviously older than my friends' parents, and since I'd already lost both of my young, healthy parents, I knew how cruel life and fate could be. I'd carried that worry of losing her right through to adulthood, but last night, hearing the doctor go on about how healthy she was, nearly made me cry with relief. Nana walked out of there with her arm in a sling and a big, broad smile on her face.

I was vaguely aware of Jack asking me a question—something about getting the starter ready for tomorrow's breads. It had already been a long morning. I looked up from the tray of scones. "I'm sorry, Jack. What was that?"

"Just asking if I should get the starter going?"

"Yes, sure, Jack, and Jack, thank you so much. You're truly a godsend."

"I know you had a rough evening, and I'm happy to help out. I just started another pot of coffee." Jack had that kind of fatherly grin that was often needed when I was having a hard day. His big cheeks rounded and it put crinkly lines around his eyes. Jack had been the find of a century. I'd been desperate to hire a decent bakery assistant, a person I could trust to be at the shop well before dawn, a person who loved to work hard (essential for a bakery) and someone who knew their way around doughs and batters. I'd gotten all three and then some. While Jack looked and even occasionally talked like someone who was more suited to life on a cargo ship or loading dock, the man could create a meringue so light it practically floated off in a cloud, and his sponge was so delicate and flavorful, it made your eyes water with joy. Jack had come with some past baggage, and admittedly, I was hesitant at first to hire him, but it had been my best business decision to date. Now he was not only a hardworking assistant, but I considered him a dear friend. And my dear friend had gotten to the bakery an hour earlier than usual because he knew I was going to be late, and he'd be doing twice the work. I arrived just before the sun cracked through the early morning clouds. Jack had already piled pastries on the trays and breads in the baskets. He was amazing.

I picked up the tray of strawberry scones and carried them to the front to put inside the counter case. Jack and I liked to make seasonal scones like apple and pumpkin in fall, cinnamon and ginger in winter and peach scones in summer. Spring was always peak season for strawberries, so Jack and I had perfected a recipe for strawberry scones that were topped with a vanilla bean glaze.

The door opened and some of the morning's cool air swooshed in along with Roberta Schubert, a longtime resident of Ripple Creek. Her husband, Harry, walked in behind her holding a bag of groceries from Roxi's market. When Nana landed in the small mountain town as a young, single mom desperate to find a community to accept her and her child, she never expected to find such a loving group of people. The town was inhabited mostly by artists, people who loved to live outside the parameters and constraints of city living, and there was no more beautiful place on earth than Ripple Creek. (At least in my opinion.) Nana was part of the first generation, and my mom and her friends were in the second. Roberta had been born in her mom's small cabin. Her mom, Eleanor, an old friend of Nana's who eventually died of heart disease, had immigrated from the British Isles, and for years she ran a teahouse with proper British tea and scones until her health issues got in the way.

Roberta and Harry were in their early sixties, and both of them were still spry and active. Roberta was almost a little too energetic. She moved erratically and quickly and always spoke way louder than necessary, while Harry was far more subdued and quiet. Harry was also much more pleasant than his wife.

"Morning, Roberta and Harry." This morning, Roberta was wearing one of her signature floral print blouses that was so bright, it hurt my tired eyes. "What can I get you both? Just carried out a fresh tray of strawberry scones." I knew I'd made a misstep the second the words left my mouth. I'd forgotten that Roberta was not a fan of what she referred to as the sugar-drenched calamity that Americans called scones. Her instant face crinkle and Harry's slight flinch assured me I was now going to get an earful. I'd heard her speech before and found it easiest to just smile and nod at her lecture.

"Dear Scottie," she said with a condescending grin. At least she started the tirade with "dear." "Those strawberry-dotted pastries on that tray are not worthy of the scone title. I'm sure they're perfectly tasty, just like a cookie or brownie, but they are as far from being a scone as that lemon meringue pie over there."

Harry looked around the bakery as if my décor interested him. He was embarrassed by his wife's abrasiveness, but I didn't mind. I'd heard the same speech many times.

"Yes, I know your mother, Eleanor's, scones were the true, traditional scone, the kind they serve at tea in England, and those are delicious. Now, can I interest you in a cheese Danish?"

Harry perked up at the topic change. "Yes, I'd love one."

"And you, Roberta?" I asked.

Roberta's face suddenly rounded in glee. "I guess I haven't

told you my big plans. I'm afraid you might not be too happy about them."

"Now, dearest, it's only a germ of an idea, so far," Harry muttered and avoided eye contact with her as he said it.

"What idea?" I was far too tired to work up any enthusiasm for the chat, so I just plastered on a polite smile and feigned interest.

Roberta rolled her lips in, apparently trying to slow the big announcement. "I'm going to reopen my mother's tea shop," she blurted bombastically as if there was a large audience to hear it instead of one very tired baker.

My smile stayed there, same position and size. "Very nice. I think the town will love that."

"Of course they will, and please, no hard feelings if I end up stealing some of your customers."

"Roberta, dear, the idea is still in the early stages, and Scottie's Bakery is extremely popular. I hardly think it'll be a problem for her."

"I'll get that Danish." I walked over to the pastry shelf.

Roberta continued, unfortunately. "It's more than a germ of an idea. I've already spoken to Brenda Walton about her tiny cabin at the end of town. She's moving to the city, and it'll be the perfect place for my business." A teahouse in town might bite into some of my business but then Jack and I were occasionally so swamped with customers, it would be nice to have another shop take some of the overflow.

Two women walked in, visitors most likely heading up to the resort to get in the last few weeks of skiing before the season officially ended. They walked straight to the strawberry scones, which caused Roberta to grunt in frustration. "If you want to try traditional scones, I'll be selling my homemade British scones with clotted cream and strawberry jam at my yard sale this weekend." She smacked Harry none-too-gently on the shoulder, and it startled him. "Harry, give them a flyer."

Harry slid the grocery bag onto his arm and fished in his trouser pockets. He pulled out a half sheet of paper with all the details of the yard and scone sale. Harry was a shy, reluctant sidekick. He handed the paper to one of the women, and she shoved it unceremoniously into her purse.

"We'll have two strawberry scones," the woman said.

I hadn't looked Roberta's way, but I could just imagine steam coming out of her ears. "Excuse me, but we were here first," Roberta said rudely. Not the best way to coax people to your yard sale.

The woman placed a hand against her chest. "My apologies. I thought you were finished. Please, go ahead."

Roberta lifted her chin and tugged down on her colorful blouse. She was always abrasive but truly in prime form this morning. I was sure if the women had ordered blueberry muffins instead of scones, Roberta would have allowed them to continue their purchase.

"Actually, I need to get home and start my scones. Harry, pay for your Danish. I'll meet you at the car."

Harry looked uncomfortable and contrite as he paid for his pastry. "I'm sorry about all that, Scottie. You know how she gets when there's an idea in her head. I'm sure your scones are wonderful."

"Enjoy the cheese Danish, Harry. And tell Roberta I plan to come to the yard sale. I'd love to try her scones. I always loved Eleanor's teahouse."

"You're too kind, Scottie. See you then."

Harry walked out, and I handed the women their scones. I

returned to the kitchen. Jack had, no doubt, heard the entire exchange, and he was holding back a smirky grin.

"Well, that was just what I needed this morning," I said.

"Whenever I see her walk in, I want to turn around and hide in the kitchen. So, she's going to open a teahouse, eh?"

"That's what she says. Oh well, good luck to her."

four
. . .

"JACK, I'm going home for my lunch break. See you soon."

Jack lifted his dough covered hand to wave me off. The afternoon sky was a vivid blue, not unusual for this time of year, but there was still a crisp bite in the air. I'd gotten a second wind after a cup of strong coffee and a late morning customer rush, but now, sitting in the warm, cozy interior of my car, my lids grew heavy and dreams of falling into bed floated through my head. I'd told Nana that I would be home for lunch to check on her. Hannah spent all morning with her, but she had a dentist appointment at one.

I was surprised to see Dalton's ranger truck in the driveway when I turned down our street. Bright, Popsicle-colored tanagers flitted about the orange slices Nana had placed out for the spring migrators. For the next month, we'd see a rainbow of colors flying through our yard. Nana's place was a traditional stop on their journey to summer breeding areas, and she made sure to supply them with all the calories required for a long flight. Even with one arm out of commission, Nana had managed to fill all the feeders and set the birds up with fresh fruit and grape jelly.

I parked and walked inside. Dalton was at the kitchen table with Nana. They were both eating sandwiches. Without thinking, I blurted out my disapproval. "Nana, you shouldn't be using that arm at all today. You should be resting."

Nana lifted her brows to let me know I'd just embarrassed myself. "I know. That is why Dalton kindly offered to drop by and make me lunch. And it's a delicious sandwich, Dalton," she gushed. Sometimes it seemed that some of my crush had brushed off on Nana. She adored Dalton, and he could do no wrong. Even his simple cheese and mayo sandwiches were apparently beyond compare.

"Oh, sorry. Thanks, Dalton. I'd planned to make her some lunch when I got home, so I appreciate it."

Dalton always looked extra handsome in his uniform. "I could make you a sandwich, too," he said.

"No. That's all right. You two carry on. I've got a yogurt in the fridge." I busied myself chopping some walnuts to drop into the yogurt while they continued their lunch behind me.

"So, where were we?" Nana asked. "That's right. You haven't said. How are you feeling about Crystal's move to New York?" Dalton had been in a long engagement with Crystal Miramont, a member of the wealthy Miramont family. They owned the big resort and half the mountain. He broke it off, and there was a lot of turmoil and drama with the breakup, but Crystal had finally moved on to someone else—a rich East Coast lawyer. Since Dalton and I rarely spoke these days, I got most of my updates from Nana.

"Uh, I'm happy for her. This guy is more her style, and now

her father has turned off his wrath and threats toward me because he much prefers her new fiancé."

I turned around with my yogurt. "They're already engaged?" I asked. I didn't bother myself too much with Crystal gossip. The two of us were never friends, not even close, but I was sure she'd only been dating the new man for a few months. I was standing in a tiny kitchen with their conversation happening at the table, so I couldn't very well just eat my yogurt and ignore them.

Dalton chuckled. "I'm sure Crystal put the bug in his ear early on. After all, she has a designer wedding gown waiting in the closet, ready to go." Dalton finished his sandwich. "Well, Evie, as always, it's been a pleasure."

"Thank you so much for making my sandwich, Dalton. And remember, my door's always open."

Dalton glanced at me and then just as quickly pulled away his gaze. "Good seeing ya, Scottie. Let's hope this beautiful weather continues." He walked out so quickly it almost seemed my presence had scared him off.

"You could try to be more friendly," Nana said. "After all, you're the one who broke his heart."

I stared at her over my spoonful of yogurt. "I'm the one who broke his heart? You of all people—the woman who had to sit with me and wipe my runny nose and feed me warm oatmeal cookies because I was in a meltdown about how much I loved Dalton and how he was never going to return that love."

"And when he did, you told him you didn't want him."

I finished my spoonful of yogurt. "Oh my, I think those pain pills might be messing with your sense of reason."

"I didn't take my pills."

I opened my mouth to protest, but she held up her hand to stop me.

"They make me dizzy, and I don't think that's a good thing when I'm trying to stay up on two feet. I don't need the other arm broken."

"All right. As long as you're not in too much pain."

She scoffed. "Please. You forget I was born in a different era when you gritted your teeth through pain. I once had three cavities filled with no Novocain."

"That's crazy. I won't let the dentist start until he's got my mouth so numb you could set my lips on fire and I wouldn't notice." I dug back into my yogurt. There was still a lot to do at the bakery, and I wanted to get back.

Nana seemed to be smiling as she chewed her sandwich.

"What's going on?" I asked. "You look like you're planning something."

She wiped her mouth. "That's because I am. I'm going to pull out my old matchmaker's handbook and set Dalton up with Tanya Hammond."

I sucked in some yogurt, coughed and drank a sip of water to clear it. "Tanya Hammond? Roxi's niece?" Tanya had moved to town after she lost her job in the city. She was working at the market. We were close in age, but we hadn't really had a chance to get to know each other. She seemed nice enough. She was definitely pretty, with a tall, athletic figure. "I don't know if she's Dalton's type. And since when do you have a matchmaker's handbook?"

"Well, I'm speaking metaphorically, of course. The handbook is up here." She pointed to her temple. "Why don't you think she's his type? She's very pleasant and pretty."

I shrugged. "I don't know. She might be a little too—I don't know—boring maybe."

"You hardly know her." Nana set down her sandwich. "Hard to eat with one hand. It almost seems as if you're jealous." Nana was good at handing out a minor, easy to miss comment and then following it with something explosive.

My laugh might have been too abrupt. "Jealous? Why would I be jealous? I'm dating a wonderful man."

"Yes, you are, and I think you should be happy for Dalton's new relationship with Tanya."

"Uh, I think you're getting a little ahead of yourself, Miss Matchmaker."

"My plan will work."

I sighed. "Well then, best of luck to you." I focused back on my yogurt, and, at the same time, a little voice in my head was asking, "What on earth, Scottie? Are you actually jealous?" I brushed the whole thing off as being far too tired to think straight.

five
. . .

I GOT BACK to the bakery. Jack looked up from the trays of peanut butter cookies he'd been portioning out. Jack and I had spent months perfecting an old-fashioned peanut butter cookie recipe, and the results of our hard labor were soft, chewy, decadent peanut butter cookies that held up when dunked in milk.

"You look exhausted, Jack. I selfishly forgot that you got to work an hour early to make up for my tardiness. I can finish those cookies. Instead of a lunch break, take the rest of the day off. I'll finish up and do prep."

"But you're the one who only got a few hours of sleep," he said. "This old, wrinkly face always looks tired. Maybe I should get a cheek and eyelift," he said with a chuckle.

"I think you're very handsome just the way you are, and those lines on your face show wisdom, not age."

"Have I ever mentioned that you're the best boss I've ever worked for?"

"You have, but I don't ever mind hearing it. Really, Jack, the shop is slow this afternoon. Go home and put your feet up. You deserve it."

Jack reluctantly took off his apron. "Putting these tired feet up does sound good. If you're sure?"

"I'm sure. Have a good afternoon. I'll see you tomorrow."

Jack hung up his apron and went to the office to get his things. "How is your grandmother doing? Is she in a lot of pain?"

"If she is, she doesn't show it. Not surprising for Nana. She's doing well. Thanks for asking." I walked him out.

Cade stepped in as Jack was leaving.

"Hey, Rafferty, how's it going? I'm halfway through your latest novel, and I'm embarrassed to admit, this one makes me check twice that my doors and windows are locked before I get in bed."

"Then my plan has worked. Take care, Jack."

I had to gather a set of nerves that were bouncing all over the place at the sight of my tall, dark and very handsome boyfriend. We'd left on rough terms the night before. The evening had started out so well that it made the bad ending feel even worse.

"How is Nana?" Cade asked.

"She seems to be doing fine. Didn't even bother with her pain medication. It takes a lot to slow down my grandmother." I decided to leave off the part about her having lunch with Dalton. Cade preferred to not hear about him … ever.

"That's good to hear." Cade looked pointedly at my neck and then his face dropped in disappointment. "You don't have to keep it or wear it. Like I said—jewelry selection is not a skill I've mastered. And I suppose that stems from lack of experience. I've never had a reason to shop for jewelry."

I reached to my neck instinctively. "I love the necklace, Cade, really. I never wear jewelry to the bakery. It's a hazard and not exactly good food safety protocol. And I think you underestimate your jewelry-picking skills."

Cade nodded. "Of course, that makes sense. Boy, I just keep stepping in it, don't I? Sounding like a sorry sap and all that."

I motioned for him to follow me into the kitchen. He walked through the small gate on the counter. We reached the kitchen, and I spun around, threw my arms around his neck and kissed him. His hazel eyes looked green under the bright lights.

"Uh, pardon me, Miss Ramone, but is this considered food safety protocol?"

"Nope, but sometimes you've got to break the rules." I kept my arms around his neck and gazed up at him. "I'm sorry, Cade. It was such a perfectly lovely evening, and somehow things went awry. And then I had to leave in a frantic rush."

"I'm sorry I got so whiny about your secret. Whiny is not a good look on me."

"I agree." I dropped my arms. "Brownie?" I asked.

"Do you really need to ask?"

I grabbed a brownie for him. He pulled up a work stool.

"I really wasn't keeping it a secret for any particular reason. You see, that money—I don't think about it much, and I rarely use it because—it's sort of tainted. I don't mean that it was ill-gotten gains or anything like that. It's just that the money, well—"

"You were orphaned. That money came to you because both your parents died." We were already at that point in our relationship where we could finish each other's thoughts.

"Exactly. The money came out of a terrible tragedy and broken heart. I was young, and Nana filled the void, but I still felt their loss keenly."

The shop door opened. I hopped up to help the customer. It was Roxi's niece, Tanya. Roxi had been working hard to get the two of us to start a friendship, but I had so little time for a social life, I was lucky when I got a few minutes to talk to my good friend, Esme, and her shop was right next door.

"Hi, Tanya."

She had a beautiful smile and big green eyes to go with it. "Hey, Scottie."

"Let me guess, Roxi ran out of fresh cookies at the sandwich counter."

Tanya nodded exuberantly causing her blonde ponytail to fall over her shoulder. "You guessed it. Your cookies are so delicious. I love them all. Chocolate chip are still my favorite, but those peanut butter cookies …" Her eyes drifted up. "They melt in your mouth."

"That's what Jack and I were going for. How many cookies do you need?"

"Roxi wants a dozen more—mixed but heavy on the chocolate chip."

"Coming right up." I started to fill a box with cookies.

Cade walked out from the kitchen.

"Oh hello, Cade," Tanya said cheerily. She seemed to add an extra sparkle to her smile.

"Hey, Tanya," Cade said.

I looked up from my task. "Do you two know each other?" I asked, then rolled my eyes. "Of course you do, since Cade shops at the market."

"We met last week, and it was Tanya's first day on the job." Cade was adding his own little dash of sparkle as he tossed a smile her way.

Tanya put her fingers to her mouth in a coy gesture. "I still

London Lovett

won't forgive myself for putting mustard on your sandwich when you specifically asked for no mustard."

"No harm done," Cade said with a casual shrug.

Tanya looked at me. "He's such a good sport. He didn't complain or return the sandwich."

I finished filling the box. I lifted my brows in surprise. "You ate a sandwich with mustard?" There were two things Cade considered vile—mustard and pickles.

"I decided to handle it like an adult," Cade said with a wink … toward Tanya.

The flirtatious moment wasn't over. "How is the newest book coming?" Tanya flipped her ponytail back off her shoulder as she asked it. Admittedly, her hair was luxuriously thick. Apparently, aside from the mustard mistake, Cade and Tanya had been talking about his work.

"Well, the biggest problem with getting to a point in your career where they offer you an advance on just a synopsis is that you get paid, but the entire body of work is still tangled up in your braincells."

Tanya made a cute little wince-y face. "That does sound stressful. Is that how writer's block—"

Cade put up his hand. "Don't say those two words out loud, please."

Tanya laughed. It was a good laugh—darn it.

"Here are the cookies," I said a little too abruptly. "I'll put them on Roxi's account."

Tanya took the box. "Thanks, Scottie, and as always, it was great seeing you, Cade." She walked out. Cade had the audacity to watch her walk away, or maybe he was innocently clueless. She was very pretty with an athletic build, like me.

I cleared my throat, and he turned around. "Well, that was adorable," I said cattily.

"She's a nice girl, and ... oh, wait—is that jealousy? Hmm, you know, the emotion I'm constantly being accused of?"

"You were doing the Mr. Charm act solely for my benefit, weren't you?"

"It's possible. How'd that feel?"

"Not good."

"Right."

"Nana has it in her head that she's going to match Tanya up with Dalton," I said for no apparent reason except that it was obviously still stuck in my craw.

"Good for Nana," Cade said.

"I don't know if she's his type." I looked up and found Cade staring at me with an annoyed brow arch.

"What? I just think that Nana should stay out of it." I didn't realize I was digging myself into a hole. I was blaming my lack of sleep.

"Right. Well, I've got to get back to work," Cade said curtly.

"Wait, are you mad again?" I was really a lunkhead today.

"I'm fine. Gotta get to that book. It's not going to write itself." He swished out the door without another word.

I stood there staring at his retreating back and replayed the last few minutes in my head. "Well done, Scottie," I muttered. I plucked the biggest brownie off the tray and carried it to the back to devour.

six
. . .

I MUDDLED through the rest of the afternoon and almost regretted letting Jack leave early. Almost. But he really needed it. He joked about always looking tired due to wrinkles, but there were dark rings under his eyes. Even his ramrod straight posture had started to slouch wearily.

I finished the prep for tomorrow morning and should have gone straight home to rest. The only problem with that was I knew, too well, if I rested, I'd fall asleep and then I'd mess up my entire sleep schedule with a big midday nap. Hannah had texted that she was at Nana's making some tea, and that they were going to sip tea and read books. That meant I had some free time, and I desperately needed to talk to my friend, Esme. Esme owned Nine Lives Bookshop next door. We both started our businesses around the same time, and we became instant friends.

There were a few customers helping themselves to the free tea Esme offered each day on a brass cart with wheels. Two of her cats, Earl, a giant gray tabby, and Salem, a shiny black cat with amber eyes, trotted over to greet me as I stepped inside. I crouched down to give Earl a scratch behind his ear and Salem a rub under her chin, their respective favorite spots.

"Scottie, how is your grandmother?" Esme asked as she walked across with a stack of books. In a small town like Ripple Creek, everyone knew big news like Nana's broken wrist almost instantly. I'd been groggy enough all day I might have been the one to tell her in a text. I just wasn't thinking clearly enough to remember. Esme was tall, five-foot-ten, so she had no problem pushing the stack of books she held onto a top shelf in the hobby section.

I helped her by hanging on to a few books while she straightened out the spines. "She's doing well, thanks."

Esme took the last few books from my hand and pushed them onto the shelf. The bell rang up at the checkout desk. I followed her to the front. A man was standing at the desk with a stack of three books, including Cade's latest novel. He always took the time to come in and sign the books for Esme when she got in a new shipment. His career had really taken off. There was even talk about a movie deal for his most recent bestseller. I was extremely proud of him, and as I thought it, I realized I didn't tell him that enough. I'd really blown it this afternoon when Cade came to visit. I'd spent a ridiculous amount of time going on and on about Dalton and Tanya. That was my reason for the trip to the bookshop. Poor Esme was always my sounding board when I was having relationship trouble. After a few bad relationships, Esme had resigned herself to staying alone and independent, and I had to admit she seemed happy with her choice. I was also sure if the right person walked into her life, she'd change her mind.

Esme helped the customer check out, and we both walked over to the tea cart. "It's orange and ginger," Esme said.

I took a whiff of the tea. "Yep, I'm smelling both."

Esme sighed. "Let's sit on the reading sofa. I've been shelving new books all day, and I need to give my feet a rest."

We settled onto the big, worn sofa she'd placed in one of the many bookstore alcoves. Earl joined us instantly, curled himself between us and immediately started a loud purr session.

"What's new?" She paused. "You look tired."

I nodded. "Nana and I were at the hospital until midnight, so I didn't get much sleep."

Esme crinkled her nose. "You poor thing. I'm never any good without enough sleep. I sense that this look"—she circled her finger in the air around my face—"is more than just lack of sleep."

I'd come over to spill my whole terrible confession out but suddenly realized I wasn't in the mood. Sitting on the comfy couch was making me drowsy. "It's just a little thing between Cade and me. I'm probably blowing it all out of proportion because I need sleep."

"Oh, speaking of blowing things out of proportion—" Esme moved to get up and then paused. She looked at me, biting her lip in concern. "Maybe you're not in the mood to see this."

"No, go ahead. I'm already sitting in this bubble of groggy numbness, so throw it at me."

Esme got up and returned a few seconds later with a stack of what looked like flyers. I nodded as she sat down.

"Let me guess, Roberta Schubert left a stack of flyers about her yard sale for you to hand out to customers."

"So, you've seen them. I politely took a stack, but after I read what it said, I took them off the counter."

I took hold of one. "You're a loyal friend, but I saw one and —" I stopped and read the flyer. "Oh, it seems, Roberta printed up some new ones. The one I saw wasn't quite so, hmm, what's the word?"

"Acerbic?"

"Yeah, that works." I lifted the flyer and read it aloud. "Come to Roberta's yard sale! We've got everything from clothes to antiques, and Roberta will be selling her authentic British scones. Not like the pretend ones at the bakery." I looked up. "Nice. She told me she's planning to open a teahouse, like the one her mother used to run. Only Eleanor was always pleasant. I can't say the same for Roberta."

"She mentioned the teahouse to me, too." Esme sensed that the flyer was aggravating her very tired friend, so she plucked it from my hand and tossed it aside.

"I suppose it will cut into my business, but that's all right."

Esme relaxed back and stroked Earl's soft fur. He restarted his purr motor. "I don't think it'll have any effect at all. People love your bread and baked goods. An occasional stop in a teahouse is nice, but it's not the same as fresh bread and pastries."

"You're probably right. And Harry said it was still just a germ of an idea, so it sounds like she's a way off from actually opening the place. I'm going to drop by the yard sale tomorrow and try a scone just for the fun of it. I've had a traditional British scone many times, but I want to show her there's no hard feelings. She can insult my American scones all she wants. I'm still going to bake them." I pressed a hand to my lips to stifle a yawn. "Oh my gosh, is it bedtime yet? I wish it were dark outside. That's the only excuse I need to get in bed."

Esme laughed. "Remember the days when we considered it a badge of honor if we were out past midnight?"

"That shows you how crazy people are in their twenties. I much prefer to be tucked in by the time the moon is up in that sky." I patted Earl on the head. "I think I'll head home and take a cool shower. That might help me make it until dark. As usual, thanks for lending me your ear, dear friend."

"Any time, and I hope the moon comes up a little early tonight—just for you."

seven

. . .

NANA HAD FALLEN asleep on the sofa with a magazine on her lap, and her head dropped awkwardly to the side. I knew she'd had trouble sleeping after the hospital visit, so I let her keep snoozing and tiptoed into the kitchen for a cup of tea. The smell of cinnamon filling the house must have stirred her awake.

"Button? Is that you?"

"Yes, Nana, sorry for waking you."

She groaned in pain. I put down the tea and rushed out to the front room. "Is it your wrist?" I asked.

"No, it's my neck." She rubbed it. "I got sleepy reading this magazine and decided to go lie down in my bed, but I fell asleep before I could put my plan into action."

I grabbed the heating pad from the arm of the big chair and carried it over to her. "Here, put this on your neck and shoulder," I said as I turned the pad on. "The kettle is still hot. I'll make you some tea."

A few minutes later I carried two cups of tea out to the sofa.

Nana was resting her head back with her eyes closed and the heating pad pressed against her shoulder. She opened her eyes as I sat down. "How was your day, Button?" She took hold of her teacup. "At least I broke my left wrist, so I can still function. Sort of. I really wanted to make you some macaroni and cheese tonight. You've been working so hard, and I know you didn't get enough sleep last night."

"I'll make the macaroni and cheese. You're off kitchen duty for a few weeks. Should we invite Hannah?"

Nana crinkled her nose. "You know I love dearest Hannah. She's such a good friend, but she does talk a lot of nonsense. She told me Roberta Schubert was on a crusade to ruin your business because you don't serve proper English scones. So silly."

"Actually, this time Hannah's gossip was mostly true." Hannah had a habit of exaggerating about everything, so we were used to her embellishments. "I'm not entirely sure if she's on a crusade to ruin my business, but she is planning to reopen a teahouse like her mom ran. She's selling her traditional scones at her yard sale tomorrow."

"Roberta will never make a go of it," Nana said. "She doesn't have her mom's wonderful charisma. Eleanor's business flourished because people loved her. I don't think the same can be said about Roberta."

"I'm not too worried. Harry and Roberta were in the shop this morning, and Harry kept reminding her it was still just in the idea phase. Anyway, Nana, I wanted to let you know that I told Cade about my wealth."

Nana winked. "It was about time. How did he react?" Nana sat forward, dislodging the heating pad. "Oh Button, you look upset. What's wrong?"

I shook my head, not realizing that my face was showing

how crummy the last twenty-four hours had been. "No, I'm fine. I told him just as I got your text, so we didn't really have time to discuss it at length, but his initial response wasn't what I expected. He seemed to think I was keeping it a secret from him, almost as if I didn't trust him with the knowledge."

"I'm sure he was just hurt. You two are getting very close—" She looked at me for agreement.

I nodded and smiled. "We are."

"Well, you were keeping a fairly important aspect of your life from him." Nana winced as she rested back.

I pressed the heating pad against her shoulder.

"Actually, that time it *was* my wrist, but leave the pad. It feels nice."

"I don't consider that part of my life important. I could see him being upset if I'd kept from him that I secretly have a son or that I was once part of a crazy cult, but having money in the bank—"

Nana raised a brow at me.

"All right, having a significant amount of money in the bank—money that I rarely think about or use—that's not that big of a deal."

"Well, it's a life-changing amount, Button, but I know you don't think about it much. Now that it's out in the open, I'm sure you'll be able to talk about it more. I'm sorry my text ended your night on a rough edge. What else is on your mind? I sense there's more."

I could never sneak my feelings past Nana. Even when I was sure I was doing a good job hiding them. But now that she'd asked, I was glad to talk about it. It had been sticky like glue in my conscience all day.

"For a brief moment last night, I thought Cade was going to

propose. It turned out he'd bought me a necklace, but there were a few fretful moments when I thought he'd bought me a ring."

Nana sipped her tea and handed it to me to place on the table. "Fretful. Why does that word not fit well with a possible forthcoming proposal scenario?"

"Fretful might be the wrong word. Let's just say I was more unsettled than I was giddy. I adore Cade, as you know. I'm just not sure I want to give up my independence. I almost made that mistake once before."

Nana was shaking her head before I finished. "You can't possibly compare the two situations or the two men. Jonathan was a toad, and Cade is a prince."

I laughed. "Yes, that pretty much covers it. And I know this isn't the same, but I like being my own boss and having my own business and—"

"You can have all those things and have a husband, too," she said.

"Coming from a woman who used to say if she had to choose between a bunion and a husband, she'd choose the bunion every time."

Nana chuckled softly. "Did I say that? That wasn't very nice of me. But that's only because I never met a man who made me entirely and thoroughly happy. You have that with Cade."

"No argument there, but does that all change if we get married?" I waved off the question. "Never mind. It's silly to talk about this because he didn't propose. Cade likes his independence, too, and for now, we'll carry on just like we are. It works perfectly for both of us. We still have plenty of time within our busy work schedules to get together."

Sitting on the couch with a relaxing cup of tea made my

muscles and the tension of the day disappear. My head felt heavy, and a big yawn rolled up and out.

"You poor baby, you had to stay up too late last night to take care of your clumsy grandmother. Go take a nice shower, and I'll make—" She paused and sat back with exasperation. "Darn this broken wrist."

I leaned forward and kissed her cheek. "I get to take care of you for a change, and frankly, it's about time. I'll shower and then start on the macaroni and cheese."

"Buttery breadcrumbs on top?" Nana asked as I headed to the hallway.

"I think that broken wrist calls for an extra layer."

eight
. . .

MY PROVERBIAL "BEST LAID PLANS" for the previous afternoon fell quickly apart when I could no longer fight the grogginess in my head. Nana had gone in to lay down while I prepared the macaroni and cheese dinner. While the cheesy noodles baked, I sat down on the couch and picked up the same *Mountain Living* magazine Nana had been reading. Apparently, it was an especially boring edition because, just like Nana, my head dropped awkwardly to the side, and I dozed off. I slept right through the oven timer and was woken instead by Nana shaking me. The house was filled with fragrant smoke. The double layer of buttery breadcrumbs was so singed, I had to scrape them off the top. At least they'd provided a heat barrier for the noodles below. The casserole was quite edible, and it was warm enough outside to open some windows and release the smoke, but I felt terrible about letting it burn. I had bragged about my opportunity to take care of Nana for a change, only I blew it and shirked all duties for a nap. On top of that, the nap had messed up my sleep schedule, and for a second night in a row, I stayed up way too late for a fresh, early morning start. I'd made it to the bakery on time, but I wasn't on top of my game. Poor Jack, once again, had to step into action and become the team leader.

For a Saturday, the bakery was unusually slow. It was chilly outside, but the sun was shining, so I couldn't blame the weather for the slow business. Jack was taking a coffee break, resting his tired feet, and I was rearranging trays so I could fit the nearly untouched strawberry scones in a more prime location.

I lifted a plate of chocolate chip cookies out of their usual spot, and as I straightened, I bumped my head hard on the top edge of the case. I reached up instinctively to rub the top of my head, and in doing so, my hand hit the arm holding the plate of cookies. Half the cookies slid off and onto the floor.

"Darn it, darn it, darn it," I grumbled.

Jack came out from the kitchen. "What happened? I heard a thud."

"Bumped my head and then dropped some cookies." I pointed out the pile of broken cookies on the floor. "Ever have one of those days when you just want to curl up in bed and—I don't know—hug a teddy bear or suck a thumb?"

Jack smiled graciously. "I'll clean up the mess. And yes, I've had those days more times than I'd like to count. Not so many now that I'm here at the bakery."

I smiled back. "You're the best, Jack." I touched the top of my head and winced. "Ouch, there's already a bump."

"Go put some ice on it." He glanced at the case. "What were you trying to do?"

"I wanted to display the scones more prominently. No one is buying them."

"I'll move some things around. Go get the ice. Oh, and while I do love a good teddy bear, I never, ever suck my thumb. Used to do it as a little tyke, so my mom rubbed cayenne pepper on my thumb to keep it out of my mouth."

My chin dropped. "That borders on—"

He nodded. "Don't forget, I grew up in a time when seatbelts were ignored and a bike helmet would have made you the laughingstock of the neighborhood."

"You're right. The cayenne doesn't sound all that bad. I'm going to get that ice. Thanks for cleaning up my mess."

The door opened just as I sat with the ice pack on my head. I heard Esme's voice out front. I held the ice in place and walked out to see her.

Her eyes rounded. "What happened?"

"Just stood up at the wrong time. My depth perception and all other faculties are still lacking proper sleep. Brownie?" I asked.

"Yes, please."

Jack was sweeping up the cookie mess, so I plucked a large brownie off the tray and handed it to her. Usually she insisted on paying, but today, I waved off her card. "Please. You'll be doing me a favor. As you can see, we're still pretty stocked. Don't know what's going on."

Esme bit her lip and smiled weakly at me.

"Uh-oh, what's going on?" I asked.

"It's nothing really. My store is slow, too. I've seen a lot of people with those yard sale flyers in their hands or under their arms. Maybe everyone is over at Roberta's sale. A woman came in to buy a book for pricing antiques because she was sure she'd just bought a valuable glass lamp from Roberta for twenty bucks."

"Well, I feel better knowing it's not just my store. You're right. People might be busy at the yard sale. I'm planning to go buy one of her scones later. She takes every opportunity to insult my American-style scones, and I want to see if she has her mom's scone baking talent. I do remember eating Eleanor's scones with clotted cream after school. They were quite the treat."

Esme picked up her brownie and squinted scrutinizingly at me. "Everything else all right? I mean, other than the ice pack on the head?"

"You're referring to the dark rings under my eyes and the blank, listless stare."

Esme and Jack exchanged grins. "Yes, that's what I was referring to."

"I just need to get my sleep pattern back on track, then I'll be back to my cheery, less clumsy self." If I really thought about it, I was somewhat relieved that today had been slow in the shop.

"I better get back to the bookstore." She lifted the brownie. "Thanks for the treat."

Jack finished the cookie clean up. The ice was supposed to help the bump on my head, but it gave me an ice cream headache instead. "Jack, I'm going to pop over to the market. Roxi said she just got in some sliced almonds. We need them for next week's bear claws."

"Sounds good. Careful crossing the street," he said with a sly smile.

"All right. Got the message. I'll look both ways … twice." The fresh air seemed to be something I needed. I took a few good sips of mountain air before I walked into Roxi's store. Isabella Fromme and Colleen Johnson were standing at the counter talking to Roxi. Roxi Tuttle had moved to Ripple Creek years ago after being newly divorced. Back then, the town market was a dreary place where the shelves were stocked with items that were long past their "use by" dates, but Roxi transformed it into a fun, vibrant market offering fresh produce, gourmet cheeses and, most importantly of all, homemade sandwiches. In the summer, visitors lined up to buy them. They were the perfect accompaniment for a long hike or bike ride.

Roxi smiled at me past Colleen's wide-brimmed straw hat. Colleen and Isabella turned back to find the recipient of Roxi's smile. Colleen lifted her brow at Isabella as if they had some great secret between them, a secret that had to do with me.

I ignored the exchange. "Afternoon, ladies." I made a split business decision right then. "Everything at the bakery is half off until closing, so drop on by."

"Really?" Isabella asked. She was forty-something, and she worked up at the Miramont Resort. "I'd love to come by, but I've already eaten a—" She paused when Colleen's elbow jutted her way.

"Eaten a?" I asked.

Colleen sighed as if I'd browbeaten something out of her. "All right. We both ate one of Roberta's scones with clotted cream." It spilled out like some great confession.

"That's nice," I said, although deep down I was thinking, "So that's it, I've been pushed out of the baking top gun position with just one scone."

"So, you don't mind?" Isabella asked.

I laughed lightly to show her just how much I didn't mind. I sort of minded but didn't want them to know it. "No, of course not. I'm planning to drop by the yard sale to try a scone, myself."

The women, Roxi included, seemed to be relieved by my

reaction. "I'm so glad," Isabella said. "It's just—the scone was delicious, and I felt, I don't know, almost traitorous for enjoying it so much." They weren't the words I wanted to hear, especially with the way my day had been going.

"Roberta insists she's going to reopen a teahouse like her mom used to run," Colleen said. She'd been a local for a lot longer than Isabella, so she remembered the old teahouse. "I'm thrilled about the prospect. I used to love Eleanor's teahouse. I sure hope it won't put a dent in the bakery business like Roberta was saying."

I perked up even though I was feeling very un-perky this afternoon. "That's what she was saying, eh?" I asked and tried to force a smile.

Roxi caught my forced smile. "That's just ridiculous. You know Roberta. Always on her high horse about something. Everyone loves Scottie's pastries, cookies and cakes. The scones aren't going to replace those yummy treats. I can't even keep enough of her cookies in stock." We all glanced toward the cookie basket. Unfortunately, there were plenty of cookies in the basket this afternoon. "Well, most days. It's been slow in here all day," she explained quickly. It was sweet of her to come to my defense. "How is Evie?" she asked briskly to change the subject.

"Oh yes," Colleen said. "I heard about Evie. Is it true she's going to need surgery?"

I shook my head. "No, that's the rumor mill surging ahead without all the facts." That was one of the hazards of small-town gossip. Something as simple as a fender bender at the stop sign would eventually end up being a multi-car pileup with injuries and lawsuits. "No surgery. A few weeks in a cast and probably some physical therapy and she'll be as good as new. I came in for some sliced almonds," I said to Roxi.

"Top shelf," she said.

I nodded politely to Isabella and Colleen and was relieved that they left before I got back to the checkout counter.

"Roberta probably won't even get her idea off the ground," Roxi said. "I'll put the almonds on your tab."

"I'm not too worried about it. I actually think a teahouse would be nice. It can only encourage people to visit the town. I do think I'll slow down on the scone production for a few weeks. I've got a tray full of strawberry scones at the bakery. It was a really slow day."

"Same here. I guess everyone is busy looking for treasures at the yard sale." Roxi looked at me. "You look tired."

"So I've heard. I've been thrown off by Nana's accident, but I'll get back on schedule soon."

Roxi's expression turned sympathetic. "Give Evie a hug for me. I hope she feels better soon."

"Thanks, Roxi. If you need any goodies, half-off across the road. Otherwise, Jack is going to have a big load to carry down the hill to the soup kitchen. Unless Roberta swept through there, too, and filled their empty bellies with her *traditional* scones."

"She's never struck me as the charitable type," Roxi said with a laugh.

"Good point. See you later."

"Bye, and get some sleep, Scottie."

nine

. . .

ROBERTA AND HARRY had inherited her mom's house. It sat on a nice piece of flat land, about a half-acre, and it was surrounded by thick pine forest. The house itself wasn't too special, a one-story brick with windows that seemed far too small given the view around it, and the Schuberts hadn't done much to update it since Eleanor owned it. I was shocked, however, to see just how many things Roberta had out in her big front yard. There were a series of tables, the wobbly kind with fold-out legs you dragged out of the front closet for holidays, circling the yard, and each table was piled high with things like porcelain figurines, colorful glass vases, old clocks and delicate teacups. I recognized some of the things from Eleanor's teahouse. Sitting within the circle of tables were piles of old clothes, shoes and furniture. There were half a dozen high-back elm armchairs with upholstered seats. I walked over to the chairs and ran my hand along the smooth, carved wood on the back of a chair. The faded plum fabric on the seats carried me back to my childhood when I sat on those same chairs and fidgeted until Eleanor brought out her double-tiered tray of tiny sandwiches and cakes. I loved the flaky scones. Rich, smooth cream dripped out the sides with each bite, but my favorite treats were the triangular sandwiches made from soft white bread and filled with cream cheese and cucumber. I remembered using the ornate silver tongs Eleanor delivered with the tea set to pick up sugar cubes and drop them into the tea, one after the other, until the tea was almost too sweet to drink.

Roberta was bartering with a man about a set of garden tools. She spotted me over by the chairs and instantly gave the man the price he asked for. "Just pay Harry," she said and then zipped across to me so fast I could almost see sparks behind her heels.

"Those chairs are from the original teahouse," she said.

"Yes, I recognize them. I was just lost in a nice moment of nostalgia. Nana took me to the teahouse on my tenth birthday. I wore my favorite pink gingham-checked sundress and shiny white boots that didn't really go with the sundress but I thought they looked very chic. I was ten, after all. Your mom was always the most gracious hostess. She brought me out a special square of frosted lemon cake with a candle in it."

Instead of getting lost in the nostalgic moment, a moment that included her mom, Roberta switched subjects. "Have you tried a scone? I had to bake a whole new batch because they sold out so fast. People can't stop talking about them."

"That's wonderful."

Her lips pulled tight. She wasn't expecting a congratulatory response. I'd never had any reason to quarrel or feel at odds with Roberta, but she sure seemed intent on pushing my buttons.

"I assume you're using your mom's recipes."

Roberta shrugged. "Mostly but I've made a few adjustments to bring down costs. Ingredients weren't nearly as expensive back when my mom ran the shop."

I nodded. "I know that quite well."

Roberta laughed, but it was forced. "That's right. You're a businesswoman, too." She said it with a simpering grin as if our current roles were switched and she was the person with an up and running business and I was just a dreamer with a glimmer of an idea.

I decided to move on from the scone discussion. "Why are you selling the chairs? I thought you'd try and recreate your mom's magical teahouse."

"Not everyone likes nostalgia," she said with a nose scrunch. Her comment was a dig at my bakery where I boasted about selling goodies that brought back wonderful childhood memories.

"Actually, I don't think that's true." I was done with our unpleasant conversation. I'd done nothing to provoke her ire, but she sure wanted to raise my hackles.

"Well, are you interested?" Roberta waved her hand at the chairs.

I almost considered buying one just to hold onto the fond memories, but I had no place to put a single chair. Then it hit me. Cade had been looking for antique chairs for a pine farm table he bought for the kitchen at the manor. I hated to see the chairs end up in someone's basement game room. "Let me think about it. How much if I take all six?"

Roberta's eyes lit up. The last thing I wanted to do was make her happy after the way she'd been treating me these past few days, but I was sure Cade would be interested. And frankly, I badly needed a win with my boyfriend at the moment.

"Well, they are antique, and they do have a lot of sentimental value—"

Not enough to consider keeping them, I thought wryly.

"Tell you what, I'll take $1,200 for all six. That's two hundred a piece, and I'll throw in a free scone with clotted cream."

"Okay. I'm going to take a picture, is that all right?"

Roberta put her hand fondly on one of the chairs as if suddenly, she was feeling a connection to them. "Sure, I guess that's okay. I've got to warn you that I've had a lot of interest in these chairs all morning, so you'll want to make a quick decision."

Roberta was quite the saleswoman. Maybe she'd make a good business owner, after all. "I will."

Roberta's eyes lit up at something behind me. "Oh look, Ranger Braddock is back." Her cheeks rounded with a smug grin. "He already dropped by for a few scones. I'll bet he's back for seconds."

I looked back over my shoulder and gave Dalton a brief wave. He'd been conspicuously absent from the bakery this morning. He usually stopped in for pastries most mornings. It seemed he'd filled up on Roberta's scones.

Roberta scurried toward him. "Ranger Braddock, back for seconds?"

I turned my attention back to the chairs. I snapped a photo and sent it off with some information. "I'm probably way too sentimental to make this kind of judgment, but these six chairs used to sit in the Ripple Creek Teahouse, and my cute little bottom wriggled and fidgeted on these very chairs quite often. What do you think—for your table?"

There was no quick response, which I tried not to fret about. Cade and I hadn't spoken since yesterday at the bakery. That wasn't too unusual because we were both so busy with work, we didn't always have time to chat, but since our conversation yesterday ended on a sour note, I was feeling a little bruised about our relationship. We rarely went through extended rough patches, but this felt like one.

I mentally listed various reasons for his lack of response as I walked toward the scone table. A big chalkboard had been hung on the tree behind the table that boasted "fresh homemade scones and clotted cream. Three dollars for one and five for two." In parenthesis, beneath the prices, it said "traditional British scones."

Roberta was being quite sparing with the clotted cream, spreading on only a thin layer rather than a fluffy dollop like her mom used to serve. I couldn't blame her. Clotted cream wasn't readily available anywhere but the UK and making it from scratch was expensive and took a lot of time and patience.

It seemed Dalton had indeed returned for more scones. He was standing at the table, and Roberta was topping a scone with cream and strawberry jam. A tray of thick golden scones that resembled American breakfast biscuits sat in an array on a baking sheet. They were still so fresh, the aroma surrounded the table.

Roberta waved off Dalton's offer to pay. He spun around, mouth wide and ready to take a bite but he paused. "Scottie, uh, I stopped by for a scone."

"Yes, I understand it wasn't your first stop. I *wondered* why I didn't see you this morning."

He had the decency to look contrite. "These are pretty good. I remember eating Eleanor's when I was a kid. Guess I was feeling nostalgic."

"Me, too." I smiled at Roberta. "Just the cream, please."

"Coming right up." I didn't get the same smile or cream-slathering flourish as Dalton, but Roberta did take the time to pick the tallest, biggest scone, and she put on a nice layer of cream. "What about those chairs?" she asked.

"Not sure yet."

She held out her hand to let me know that I'd have to pay for the scone since the chairs weren't a sure thing. I handed her my money and took a bite.

Roberta crossed her arms confidently. "They're sensational, aren't they?"

"They're very good, Roberta."

"Ranger Braddock sure likes them. This is his third scone. Ranger Braddock, I've warned Scottie that her bakery is going to see some pretty stiff competition once I open the teahouse."

Dalton shot me a sympathetic smile.

"I welcome the competition." I lifted the scone in toast and took another bite. They were a little dry ... in my professional opinion.

ten

. . .

DALTON LEFT JUST after his last bite of scone. I stuck around hoping I'd hear back from Cade, so I could give Roberta a deposit on the chairs if he wanted them. One woman was spending a lot of time looking at the chairs, so it seemed there might be competition for them. I looked over some of the pretty porcelain teacups and considered buying a few for Esme's bookshop. She had several display shelves around the shop, and I thought they'd look cute on a shelf over her tea cart. There were some beautiful, hand-painted teapots as well, but there'd be no room on a shelf for those.

I picked up a cup to make sure it had no cracks and then nearly dropped it when someone bumped hard into me. I gasped and looked up. Arnie Morris, a local, splashed an apologetic look across his face. "I'm so sorry, Scottie." That was all he said, a rather curt apology, considering he nearly knocked me off my feet.

He continued on wildly, like the White Rabbit in Alice's

Wonderland, mumbling to himself and scrunching a piece of paper angrily in his fist. Arnie searched frantically around and spotted Roberta standing at the far end of the yard showing a man how to use an old coffee grinder. Arnie marched that way.

I glanced around to see if Harry had noticed a practically rabid-with-emotion man heading toward his wife, but Harry was busy talking to the woman at the chairs. And as the woman turned just so, giving me a clear view of her face beneath her straw hat, I realized it was Janice Fairburn, Roberta's sister and Eleanor's eldest daughter. Harry was smiling and chuckling and couldn't be bothered about the scene happening across the way.

I, on the other hand, was curious to know why Arnie nearly mowed me down. I mentally thumbed through some of the layers of gossip I'd absently picked up whenever Nana and Hannah were chatting over tea. Arnie, a freelance writer, was renting a small cottage from Harry and Roberta. It was their first house after they got married, and they kept it even after moving into Eleanor's house. I would be doing Nana and Hannah proud today. I moved casually to the table closest to their conversation and pretended to be interested in the stacks of old books and albums.

"First, you nearly doubled the rent, and I went along with it," Arnie snarled. "Even though you refused to cut down the tree that drops sap all over my car, and you haven't replaced the heating system like you promised. But this eviction notice—this is too much." He waved the paper as he yelled at her. Other people at the yard sale were taking notice of the confrontation, but Harry was still across the yard chatting cheerily with Janice. Not that it mattered. I'd always gotten the impression that Roberta ran the marriage. She bossed Harry around. He never seemed to mind.

Roberta took a deep breath to show Arnie she wasn't the least bit intimidated by his scornful rant. "As I've told you in the letter, I'm going to be selling the cottage. I need the money for my future business, so I'll be putting it on the market next month. I need to get painters and plumbers in there to fix the place up, so it'll sell faster." Her brows lifted and fell. "Maybe you'll want to buy it."

"That place has so many problems—no thank you."

"Well, then, I'll need you out at the end of the month."

"Where's Harry? I'll talk to him since you're so stubborn." I couldn't see how calling Roberta stubborn was going to help his case. Roberta struck me as the vengeful type. Arnie spun around; his face red with anger. "Harry! I need to talk to you!"

Harry finally pulled his attention away from his sister-in-law. He leaned over to say something to her, and Janice smiled weakly. Harry walked across to meet up with Arnie. Harry had a much kinder, gentler way about him. He said something quietly to Arnie and then walked him into the house, presumably for a more private chat.

Janice wandered over to the tables. She stopped at a small antique chest with roses carved along the sides. I walked over to join her and mostly to find out if she planned to take the chairs with her. I assumed they belonged to her as well.

"Hello, Janice, it's been a while since I've seen you," I said.

"Scottie, hello. I guess you don't see me in that wonderful bakery much. My doctor told me to cut down on sweets, so I've had to train myself to walk past your shop. It's not easy."

"I'm sorry about that, and I completely understand. Are you part of your sister's plan to reopen your mom's teahouse?"

"Me? Heavens no. I can't believe she's started this idea. Honestly, I don't think she remembers how hard our mom worked to keep that shop running. I think she'll get bored of the idea as soon as she sees how hard it is to run a business."

"She's definitely determined at the moment." I glanced back and found Roberta back behind the scone table. She had several hungry customers waiting for their treats. "I saw you looking at the chairs. I have to tell you—seeing them sent me right back to fond childhood memories in your mom's shop. Nana and I loved to visit the teahouse."

"I miss that place." A lost, glassy look filled her eyes. "After school, we'd walk straight to the shop. Mom would have a pot of our favorite cinnamon tea and a plate of tiny egg salad sandwiches waiting for us in the kitchen. We'd drop our books in her office and settle onto the work stools for our afternoon snack."

"I was looking at the chairs earlier and remembering her cute little cucumber sandwiches. And for Valentine's Day, she cut them into heart shapes."

"That's right. I used to help her cut those shapes. I had so much fun."

"Were you thinking about buying the chairs? I suppose they're partially yours."

"No, these belong to Roberta and Harry. We split everything from the shop evenly. I have six chairs in my dining room. I can't believe Roberta can part with them so easily, but she needs the money for her new, grand scheme. And listen, I know she's been telling people that she might just put your bakery out of business, but that's crazy. Everyone loves your bakery."

"She does seem focused on that as part of her business plan. I'm not sure why. I think we've got more than enough sweet tooths in town for both our shops to thrive."

"Exactly." She chuckled. "No shortage of sweet tooths. Well, I think I'm going to take this lovely box. It belonged to our grandmother, and Roberta greedily grabbed it when we were cleaning out our grandmother's farmhouse. Now, here it sits on a table at a yard sale. Not a sentimental bone in her body, that's for sure."

The front door of the house slammed, and Arnie marched down the steps, red with rage and still clutching the eviction notice in his fist. It seemed Harry wasn't able to negotiate a truce.

Cade texted as Janice carried the box to the table. It seemed a shame that she would have to pay her sister for one of their grandmother's treasures. I glanced at the text. "I like those. Text me the address. I'm taking a computer break. Can you stick around?"

"Yes, business was slow, so Jack and I got ahead on our work. I'll be here. See you soon."

I smiled as I tucked away my phone. I was pleased that he liked the chairs, but mostly, I was pleased that he didn't seem angry. His lack of response for the past fifteen minutes had worried me. Hopefully, this wonderful find would bring us right back to our usual happy place.

eleven
. . .

I HADN'T MEANT to spend my entire afternoon standing around Roberta's yard sale, but I'd started the long stay by mentioning the chairs to Cade. I'd seen many familiar and unfamiliar faces come and go, and I got to watch Roberta in action as she haggled over prices and handed out cream-topped scones. I just couldn't see her filling her mom's shoes as hostess at a teahouse. Roberta lacked all the charisma, charm and finesse that Eleanor had brought to the place. Janice would have been a far better match for the job, but she didn't seem to have any interest in it.

 Cade pulled up in the truck he'd recently bought. He'd realized a nice, heavy-duty truck was a necessity for mountain living, especially when remodeling a large estate. Today it would come in handy for carrying chairs back home. Cade's thick, wavy hair was brushed back, and he was wearing black sunglasses and a gray T-shirt. He was always attractive, but this morning, seeing him step out of his truck made my knees weak.

I was truly crazy about the man, and I never wanted to be without him. Maybe a proposal wouldn't be such a bad thing. I knocked that revelation back for now and headed toward him. Mallory Cook, another longtime resident of Ripple Creek and a good friend of Roberta and Janice, pulled up behind Cade's truck in her bright yellow Volkswagen Beetle. The soft top was rolled back, and the Rolling Stones were blasting out of the stereo. Mallory was a fun, eccentric kind of person. She was in her sixties like Roberta and Janice, but you never would have guessed it by the way she acted. Today her hair was dyed black as ink. It was quite the contrast to her fair skin and ruby red lips.

I reached Cade, and he leaned down for a kiss on the cheek. My heart went pitter-patter even at such a simple gesture. Cade was that perfect mix of sophistication, wit and humbleness that helped keep me steady on my feet, even when my heart was racing ahead with excitement.

There was probably a better place and time for what I had to say, but we'd had a rough few moments, and I wanted to talk about it, even with my neighbors and bakery customers milling about behind me arguing over prices and checking old glassware for cracks. Cade sensed I had something important to say that didn't have to do with chairs, so he pushed his sunglasses up to his head. His hazel eyes caught me off guard for a second, but I quickly found my words.

"I feel ridiculous. I just want you to know—in case you had any doubts—don't have doubts. You just strolled up to this yard sale a few seconds ago, and my knees went to jelly. My heart is still fluttering. I'm nuts about you, Cade Rafferty. So whatever stupid stuff comes out of this mouth—well—just filter out the stupid stuff, all right? I think about you a million times throughout the day, and—" He lowered his mouth and kissed me.

As usual, his kiss took my breath away. I opened my eyes, and his gaze held mine. "You did that just to stop the rambling, didn't you?" I asked.

"Okay, so it was a double-edged kiss. In my defense, I was already dying for a kiss because it had been more than twenty-four hours. Oh, and Ramone—just for the record—you make my knees jelly, too."

I playfully smacked his chest. "Come look at the chairs, and I'll give you a little backstory to go with them. These chairs used to be in an adorable teahouse. Nana and I used to go there on special occasions, and whenever my friends and I had a few extra dollars, we'd stop there after school for a pot of hot tea. Of course, we'd immediately flood our cups with cream and sugar, making it far less like tea and more like a warm milkshake, but we felt very sophisticated, pinkies in the air and all, as we sipped tea and gossiped about school."

"I wish I'd known you back in high school." Cade squinted at me. "I'll bet I would have had a crush on you."

I laughed. "Remind me to show you a few school pictures sometime. I think they'll dispel that notion right quick."

Mallory, with her new goth look (she was even wearing black jeans with silver studs) was looking at the chairs. Hopefully, she wasn't in the market for dining chairs. Mallory spotted us, and she winked at Cade. She was one of his reader fans. "There he is, my favorite author. I read in my book group that you just got a big advance for a new book." She sidled flirtatiously up next to him. "Can you give me any hints about it?"

"Not yet but I'll post a few details soon."

"I'll let the group know. They're so jealous that I get to just shoot the breeze with the dark and mysterious Cade Rafferty." She glanced across the yard. "Oh yum, Roberta made scones. Her mom used to bake the best scones." Mallory looked at me. "Remember those?"

I nodded. "I sure do, and Roberta's are quite delicious."

Mallory scooted away in jeans that might have been a size too small.

I looked at Cade. "You'll be posting details soon? I know you were struggling some with this new one. Good to hear you've got things moving."

"Oh, I don't. In fact, I was about to ask her if she could give me a few hints. I thought it might spark some ideas. I figured 'soon' was such a vague word, might as well just tack it onto the lie."

"Shameful behavior, sir."

"I agree." Cade sat down on one of the chairs. He wriggled his bottom back and forth, which made the chair wobble on its legs. "Not very sturdy."

"Well, they're quite used, which is sort of the beauty of them. Lots of history and stories to tell. And I assume you won't be wiggling around when you're sitting down to your cereal or soup."

"Nope, never for cereal and soup. I save my butt dance strictly for sandwiches and lasagna. Those are the traditional bottom wiggle dishes."

"Oh my, I think you've been staring at the blank page on your computer too long."

"I must have started three outlines, only to delete them all. I think I've been distracted thinking about us."

"I'll come over tonight with a bottle of wine and—"

"Distract me more?" he asked with a sly smile.

"Well, I was thinking more of becoming your inspiration or muse for your next book, but now that I think about it—wasn't the last one about a family who ended up buying a cabin in the woods that belonged to a nineteenth century serial killer?"

"Yes, so you probably want to rethink that inspiration idea." He took my hand and tugged me gently to sit on the chair next to his. "I would, however, enjoy the distraction. Maybe I can get all my distractibilities out in one fell swoop."

"Distractibilities? Is that even a word?"

"Probably not in that context, but I think it works for this topic." He stood up, crossed his arms and surveyed the chairs. "I like them."

"Oh good," Roberta chirped behind us. "They are wonderful, aren't they? They hold such sentimental value. But such a good deal at $1,400. And I'm so pleased to know they'll stay together as a group."

I cleared my throat to get ready for some of the same bartering I'd heard all morning. "Roberta, an hour ago you said you'd take $1,200 for all six."

Roberta fluttered her eyelashes in shock. "Did I?"

"You did."

"Well, since that time I've had numerous people inquire about them."

I shook my head. "I've been here the whole time, and aside from your sister and Mallory, I haven't seen anyone else look at them."

Right then, Mallory marched toward us. She was no longer wearing that carefree, disaffected expression she liked to wear to let everyone know that she was just breezing through life without a care in the world. She was holding one of the teapots.

It was a particularly pretty one with cobalt blue flowers and gold leaf on the trim and handle.

"Roberta, this is my great-grandmother's teapot!" she yelled.

Roberta laughed nervously. "Obviously you're mistaken. I brought it down from the attic just yesterday. It's been up there for years."

Mallory held the ornate lid on and turned it upside down. "Peters and Sons. That's the artist's mark. They were porcelain makers in eighteenth century Britain. My great-grandmother brought it with her on a boat. She wrapped it in two woolen shawls to make sure nothing happened to it because it had belonged to her mother, my great-great-grandmother. I recognize this little crack on the bottom because it looks like a streak of lightning." Her voice wavered as she spoke about the teapot. I'd never seen Mallory anything but happy. "This pot has been missing for ten years, and I turned my house, my attic, even my garage upside down looking for it. You know that because you and Janice helped me look for it. Do you know how distraught I've been thinking that this family heirloom had been handed down through generations only to be carelessly misplaced by me?"

"I'm sure that's not the same pot." Roberta tried to wave her off, but at the same time her spine stiffened and she became more defensive.

"Don't you think I'd know my own teapot? I can feel my great-grandmother's touch on this handle. I can visualize my grandmother proudly serving tea to her friends at one of the garden parties she liked to throw. This is the pot. There's no mistake about it." Mallory had tears in her eyes. "You stole this from me." She blurted the words like firecrackers and then they hung in the air collecting tension.

Cade and I had easily faded back as a mostly invisible audience. This scene was making the one with Arnie's tirade over the eviction notice seem like a summer breeze.

"I don't have to listen to this, Mallory. You're on my property, and I'd like you to leave."

Mallory hugged the pot in her arms. "Not without this and you won't get one red cent out of me. Consider this the end to our friendship."

"Fine," Roberta said coldly. "Just go."

Mallory turned sharply (as sharply as she could in her skintight jeans) and hurried back to her car.

Roberta tugged at the hem of her shirt and lifted her chin indignantly. She was trying hard to look as if the last few seconds hadn't upset her, but a stone statue would've had a hard time recuperating from what had just transpired.

"Now, where were we?" she asked.

Cade pushed his sunglasses back down. "I'll give you nine hundred for all six. Can you take a debit card?"

"Fine, and yes, I have a card reader." With that, she turned just as sharply as Mallory and marched back to her table.

I looked over at Cade with wide eyes.

Cade shrugged. "Saw my opportunity and took it."

twelve
. . .

TOMORROW WAS SUNDAY, which meant only a short morning at the bakery. We usually served warm cinnamon rolls and a seasonal muffin, and generally, we were sold out by ten. I'd managed to gain a second wind earlier, but now sleepiness gripped me again. This time I snatched an hour-long nap, and it refreshed me. I had plans with Cade this evening, and I didn't want to be yawning into my glass of wine.

Hannah and Nana were out in the front yard talking. I stretched, drank a glass of water and then pushed open the screen door to join them. Gray clouds had floated in and landed on the mountaintops like fluffy gray pillows. I could smell spring rain in the air. It was the time of year when the weather could go from bright and sunny to a fierce thunderstorm and then back to bright and sunny all within the space of an hour. I was sure those clouds were waiting to wreak their havoc in the next few hours.

Nana and Hannah became conspicuously quiet as I stepped

out onto the stoop. I was sure I heard Hannah's mention of the new teahouse. Nana smiled up at me. "Button, you're awake. We decided to talk out here. It's such a lovely day, and we didn't want to disturb you."

"It is a nice day." I motioned with my head toward the surrounding peaks. "I think a thunderstorm is on its way."

"That's what the birds have been telling me. They were filling up at the feeders, before heading off to find shelter. How was your day? You fell asleep before we could talk."

"It was fine. Cade bought six of the chairs that used to be in Eleanor's tea shop. They look great at his table."

"Those high-back elm chairs that her mother brought over from England? I love those chairs. I can't believe Roberta was selling them."

"Well, she insisted they had great sentimental value in-between her attempts to get top dollar for them."

Hannah peered up at me almost shyly. "So, were you there for the big blow up?" Nana liked the occasional round of gossip, but like Regina, Hannah thrived on it. She lived alone with a somewhat snooty cat, and talking to Nana about town gossip was always the highlight of her day.

"The big blow up? Which one?"

Hannah's chin dropped. "There was more than one? I'm talking about Mallory Cook finding her great-grandmother's long lost antique teapot sitting right out on Roberta's yard sale table with a twenty-dollar price tag on it. Mallory is letting everyone know that Roberta stole her family heirloom right out from under her nose. I remember when she lost that pot. She actually posted reward signs all over town. She was beside herself. And all that time it was sitting in her friend Roberta's house."

Nana was supporting her broken arm with her good hand, a sure sign that it was bothering her. "Nana, why don't you two come inside and sit down? I'm going to brew a fresh pot of coffee. I need a little boost. That nap was almost too long."

Hannah chuckled as she climbed the front steps. "That's the way with naps. You've got to get just enough shut-eye to refresh, but if it's too long, the rest of the day is a blur."

The women settled at the kitchen table while I made coffee. There were leftover butterscotch blondies in the cookie jar. I pulled some out and put them on a plate.

"Hmm, my absolute favorite." Hannah said the same thing about all my baked goods, but I didn't mind.

Seconds later, the kitchen was filled with the comforting aroma of coffee. I leaned against the counter as I waited for it to finish brewing.

"Well, Scottie, did you see the scuffle between Mallory and Roberta?" Hannah asked. "Robyn Keller was there, and she said it was quite dramatic. Mallory was in tears, apparently."

Nana looked over at her. "Well, wouldn't you be if you'd searched high and low for a teapot that had been sitting in your friend's house all along?"

"I sure would be," Hannah said with a decisive nod. "It all sounds like something Roberta would do. She gave Eleanor plenty of trouble growing up. She was always the obstinate one. Janice had a much better personality. And now Roberta's trying to hurt our Scottie's business with some silly notion that she'll start a new teahouse."

I suspected that they'd been talking about Roberta's plan when I walked outside.

"Don't be ridiculous, Hannah," Nana said. "A teahouse is no competition for Scottie's world-class baked goods."

My grandmother was always my biggest cheerleader and advocate. I kissed her cheek as I set a cup of coffee down in front of her. I poured a cup for Hannah and myself. A cup of coffee was just what I needed to restart my engine.

"Are you worried at all that Roberta's business will hurt the bakery?" Hannah asked, ignoring Nana's reassurance that it wouldn't. I wasn't so sure myself. She'd just been selling her scones at a yard sale, and she'd managed to cut my business down so badly, Jack had to pack up two dozen boxes to deliver to the soup kitchen.

"It won't be great for business," I said. "That's for certain. Competition is competition, and people love charming teahouses. The big questions are whether Roberta will follow through with the plan, and can she make a success of it?"

Hannah sipped her coffee and managed a fervent head shake at the same time. "I don't think she'll even get the doors open. And she certainly didn't inherit her mom's charm and grace. Like I said, Janice would have been a much better match for teahouse hostess, but I heard she's not interested."

"She's not," I said. "I spoke to her at the yard sale."

We enjoyed the aromatic coffee and a nice swath of silence for a couple minutes until a bolt of lightning lit up the kitchen. The trees began to sway with wind. "Well, here we go," Nana said. "Looks like we came inside just in time."

thirteen

· · ·

A SOMEWHAT BRUTAL spring thunderstorm ripped through our narrow valley. The wind left tree debris in the road, and torrential rain fell for about twenty minutes, followed by several minutes of pea-sized hail, covering the ground with the look of a fresh winter snow. Then the late afternoon sun poked between the two tallest mountain peaks, and the wind and clouds rushed out of the valley nearly as fast as they'd torpedoed in.

I'd planned to wear a nice dress to Cade's house, but the earlier wild weather had left a distinctive chill in the air, so I pulled on jeans and a light sweater. The short storm had coaxed earthy smells from the surrounding loamy earth, and the crisp scent of pine filled the air. There was still an inch of hail collected at the bottom of my windshield as I climbed into my car for the short trip to Cade's. I placed the wine bottle on the passenger seat and reached up to touch my new necklace. I was very fond of it.

Cade was outside the house picking up some small tree branches. Like my windshield, his patio furniture was still wearing the white beads of hail. "The weather up here sure has a short temper." He straightened, holding a branch of pine in each hand. "You're wearing the necklace."

I touched it. "Of course I am. I told you, I don't wear jewelry to work. I don't want someone biting into a muffin and breaking a tooth on a pearl." I walked right up to him, close enough that our toes touched.

He tossed aside the branches he'd just picked up and pulled me into his arms. I was still holding the bottle of wine, but we managed a good and proper kiss. The scent of his soap and aftershave filled my senses.

"Have I ever told you I love the way you smell?"

Cade chuckled. "That's probably the number one requirement for a successful relationship, and also the number one reason why I don't eat garlic before a date."

I was reluctant to step out of his embrace. For a good twenty-four hours, it felt as if the two of us were walking in different dimensions and nothing was lining up between us, but we'd found each other again and nothing made me happier.

"Shall we open the wine?" I asked.

"Sounds like a plan. And we can drink it sitting on the new chairs. I have to warn you, they're a little wobbly from wear." We walked inside and headed into the kitchen.

For his restoration project, Cade had tackled the garden, the patio and some of what would have been referred to as reception rooms in the house, but the kitchen was still a mix of old cabinetry and counters. He'd fixed all the broken cabinet doors, so they no longer fell into your hand while you reached inside for a cup or box of crackers, and he'd added a new stove and oven. The new appliances made the shabbiness really stand out, and at the same time, I'd grown rather fond of the mix of old and new. It had a certain appeal—the historical charm that made you know the walls had stories to tell and the convenience of being able to cook a dish of lasagna without it burning black on one side while staying raw on the other. That had happened. The only edible part was right down the center of the dish.

Cade had filled bowls with nuts and pretzels. I sat down on one of the chairs, gave it a quick wiggle and then reached for a handful of nuts. "Like being in an old pub. We just need the salty ocean air wisping around outside and a few drunken fishermen singing a sea shanty." I wiggled the chair again. "Wobbly or not, I love these chairs."

Cade carried the opened bottle of wine and two glasses over to the table. He set them down. I sighed. "You just ruined my pub vision."

"Well, we could drink the wine from dented pewter mugs, but I don't have any pewter mugs, dented or otherwise." Cade poured us each a glass. "Just pretend its ale with a big foamy top." Cade sighed. "Man, I wish it was ale with a big foamy top. I confess, I spent a lot of time in century-old pubs on my last book tour through Europe. You meet a lot of fun people, and as an author, there's nothing I like better than meeting colorful characters."

"Speaking of characters," I started and then regretted it, so I shut down the question. But Cade knew what I was about to ask.

"I started an outline today that I like or at least I haven't deleted it yet."

I clapped a few times quickly. "Does your favorite, loving, adoring superfan get to hear the inside scoop?"

Cade grabbed a handful of nuts. "Yes, and when I see Mallory, I'll tell her all about it."

I threw an almond at him, which stuck to his sweater so he picked it off and ate it. "That was quite the scene today. So, Mallory lost a treasured heirloom, and she turned the town inside-out looking for it, and her friend Roberta helped with the search, all the while knowing full well that the heirloom was sitting in her own house. That is some Twilight Zone-style stuff. Roberta seems intense. While I was paying her for the chairs, she mentioned that you were upset about the prospect of her starting a teahouse because it would be competition for the bakery."

I laughed. "That's all a conflict she's created in her own mind. And she's definitely getting ahead of herself since the teahouse is still only in the idea stage."

"So, you are worried about it?" he asked.

I blew a raspberry at him because I knew he was teasing. "Subject change. I've had Roberta Schubert up to here all day." I tapped my forehead with the side of my hand.

"Fair enough. How's Nana?" Cade asked.

"She's doing much better. She's frustrated that she can't cook and do all the chores she normally does. I was a big shot, and I told her it was my turn to take care of her for a change, then I promptly fell asleep and let a tray of macaroni and cheese burn in the oven."

"It's the thought that counts," he said with a wry grin. "I was thinking we should plan a vacation this summer, maybe Greece or Italy."

"That would be really nice. Hopefully, I'll hire some good summer help."

"And don't worry, I won't use the romantic European setting to frighten you off with a marriage proposal."

I stopped mid sip and set my glass down. I stared at him unsure how to respond.

His mouth tilted slightly up on one side. "Oh, Ramone, I know you better than you know yourself. You don't think that I noticed the look of abject horror on your face when you thought I might be hiding an engagement ring behind my back? I admit it took the wind out of my sails a bit, and I wasn't even sure I should give you the necklace."

I reached over and took his hand. "That was just me reacting to the idea of marriage. I'm like a Pavlovian dog when I hear the word *wedding*, only instead of it sending me into a daydream about flower bouquets and frosted cakes, it sends me into a panic attack. But you're not the cause of that reaction. Trust me. It's my breakup from Jonathan—his whole family, his mother, especially, were so vicious to me afterward, it left me scarred, and I vowed never to commit to anyone again. But I had some time to reflect after my initial reaction, and I wouldn't be averse to the notion at all, Cade."

"'I wouldn't be averse to the notion' wasn't quite the resounding declaration of affection and commitment you think it was."

"Oh, c'mon, give me a break. I'm trying here."

Cade chuckled. "Just teasing. It's all right. I think both of us will know when to take that next big step, and frankly, why is it always on the man? It's a decision we should make together."

"Not quite as romantic as a surprise ring, but I like the way you think, Mr. Rafferty." We lifted our glasses for a toast to our new pact.

fourteen

. . .

A NORMAL SUNDAY would start with a line of people down the sidewalk, locals and weekend visitors, waiting for their fresh-from-the-oven cinnamon rolls. Jack and I had expanded the Sunday morning offerings by adding caramel pecan rolls bursting with nuts and brown sugar filling. The line was considerably shorter than usual, which was disappointing. At least Dalton had returned.

Everyone always let him skip to the front of the line whenever he was in uniform. He was the first through the door. He looked pointedly back at the small group behind him and then turned back to me with a questioning look.

"Roberta mentioned that she'd be selling scones again today for the last day of the sale," I told him.

"Well, the scones were good—" he started.

"Yes, Roberta made sure to let me know you were a return customer."

Dalton tried to look contrite, but it was too much of an

afterthought. "I'll take one cinnamon roll, please. I don't think my arteries would appreciate another day of clotted cream."

I handed him the warm roll on a napkin and added a laugh. "If you only knew how much butter goes into these cinnamon rolls—let's just say—you're still not doing your arteries any favor."

"Shh, we just won't tell them."

Dalton took his cinnamon roll to one of the small tables near the window. Jack had the morning off. He'd decided to go fishing, and he'd earned the break. I finished with the handful of customers in the bakery and then joined Dalton with a roll of my own. I had to admit, the teahouse threat was starting to feel real. Roberta was just selling her scones at a yard sale, and she'd taken a chunk of my business.

I picked at the roll. "Do you think I need to be worried?" I asked Dalton.

"People aren't going to give up eating your baked goods, Scottie. There's nothing like 'em. And Roberta is still a long way off from getting a business up and running. She told me the yard sale was part of her financial plan to make money for the business. It was hard not to chuckle when she said it. It reminded me of my plan to mow lawns so I could buy a bicycle. A yard sale is hardly a financial plan. I talked to Harry briefly yesterday. He's always much more lowkey than Roberta. It's almost hard to see how the two of them ever matched up. Harry said that Roberta gets big ideas in her head, but she never follows through."

"Maybe she'll just sell scones from her front yard," I suggested.

"She'd still need a business permit." He finished a bite of cinnamon roll. "How's Evie?"

"Good. I think the pain is almost gone, and now the wrist just needs to heal."

Dalton was holding back a smile.

"What? Seems like you've got something on your mind, Ranger Braddock." We hadn't had such a nice, friendly conversation in a long time. I missed our chats.

"Evie has this crazy matchmaker scheme—me and Roxi's niece, Tanya." He was trying to pooh-pooh the idea like it was just a silly plan, but I sensed he was brushing it off prematurely.

"Well, what do you think?" I asked. "She's very pretty, and she has a nice personality. Admittedly, I haven't talked to her all that much. I think Roxi is disappointed that I haven't taken her more under my wing and made friends with her, but I've got Esme and Jack and …" I stopped.

Dalton raised a brow at me. "I used to be part of that chain, didn't I?" He looked down at his plate. "I miss our friendship."

"Me, too," I said, but with apprehension. Renewing our friendship would not sit well with Cade, and I had to put him first. "Let's just agree that we can have chats like this when we happen to end up together in the same place. That whole 'pretending we don't have a nice history together when we see each other' feels icky, for lack of a better word."

Dalton nodded. "Agreed."

Two women walked in. They were from out of town. One woman was busy gobbling one of Roberta's scones. She licked clotted cream off her finger and moaned about how delicious it was. Dalton, again, was holding back a smile.

"All right, that's enough," I told him. "Just finish your Scottie Ramone cinnamon roll."

The woman's friend ordered a pecan bun and showed it to

her friend, who'd already finished the last crumb of scone. "These are far better," she bragged and took a big bite as they walked out.

I looked over at Dalton. "I guess that's one point for Roberta and one for Scottie."

The front door swung open hard enough to make my *Open* sign swing back and forth like a pendulum. "Ranger Braddock, there you are. I saw your truck and thought I'd find you in here." It was Mallory. Her hair was still inky black, but she'd forgone the studded jeans and red lipstick. "I have a crime to report." She marched over and sat down across from him.

Dalton wiped his mouth with his napkin. "What's happened?" he asked calmly, even though Mallory was all worked up.

"I want to report a robbery. Something very valuable of mine was stolen."

It was my turn to hold back the amused grin. I knew exactly which item she was talking about.

Dalton sat up straighter and cleared his throat. "When and where did this robbery occur?"

"The item, my great-grandmother's teapot, was stolen from my house and right out from under my nose … ten years ago," she added casually.

Dalton stared at her, apparently trying to decide if she was joking or not. I knew too well that she was quite serious.

"I found the stolen teapot at Roberta's yard sale. She must have stolen it one day when I wasn't looking. We were good friends." She scoffed. "Obviously, not anymore." It was rare to see Mallory in such a huff. The stolen teapot fiasco had really gotten under her skin.

"With all due respect, Miss Cook, if you've found the teapot, then there isn't a lot for me to do. I'm glad you got it back."

Mallory sat up sharply, and Dalton leaned back slightly to get ready for the tirade that seemed to be bubbling up her throat. "Not a lot you can do!" she said loudly. "I can't even begin to describe the anguish and torment I went through over the loss of that teapot. And all that time, my supposed friend, Roberta, knew I was in despair. I want her arrested for theft. I will gladly file a complaint if necessary."

Dalton put on his polite, empathetic expression. I'd seen him use it before on people who were up in arms about some mishap or another; usually it had to do with a car accident and rarely a lost teapot, but it always worked. Mallory's shoulders relaxed some.

"I'm afraid there are some limitations on charging people with past crimes, and ten years is a long time for a stolen teapot. Now, mind you," he said quickly before she could puff up like an angry bird again, "what Roberta did was wrong, very wrong, and I'm going to have a word with her about it. But that's about all I can do. I'm just glad you've got the piece back. I'm sorry you had to go through so much stress over it."

I placed a cinnamon roll on a napkin and walked over to Mallory. "Here, it's on the house."

Mallory took a deep breath. "Well, this is disappointing, but thank you, Scottie. The cinnamon roll will help soften the blow." She got up. "Thanks for listening to my complaint," she said to Dalton and left the store.

Dalton looked up at me.

"Don't thank me. Thank the cinnamon roll," I said with a laugh.

Dalton got up to leave. "I'm glad we had that talk, Scottie. And now, I'm going to head out into our very odd town and see what other scandals, past and present, need my attention."

I watched him walk out and nodded to myself. "Yep, he's still something else."

fifteen

. . .

JACK STOPPED by the bakery as I was cleaning up for the morning. Normally, we sold out of cinnamon rolls by ten and then I closed the shop and had the rest of the day off. There were still two dozen rolls left on the trays.

Jack perused the leftovers and looked at me with a shrug. "Just not our week," he said glumly.

"I guess everyone is enamored with Roberta's scones. I thought they'd at least be in for the cinnamon rolls this morning. I can't believe everyone flocked over to her yard sale for another scone. They're tasty, but—gosh—I don't know, Jack. Are we in trouble here?"

"I don't think so. In fact, I came in to show you this." He pulled out a flyer. "It was on my car's windshield."

I shook my head as he unfolded it. "I've already seen Roberta's flyers."

"This isn't from Roberta." He handed it over. A delicious looking chocolate donut with sprinkles was at the top of the flyer. "Come to Donut World's grand opening at the Miramont Resort. Donuts half off, this weekend only."

"Hmm, that might be more of an explanation than the scones. I mean who doesn't love a delicious donut, and especially one that's half off?" I felt slightly relieved. As much as I'd been brushing off the notion that Roberta's teahouse would compete with my bakery business, I was starting to fret about the lack of customers, and this morning had really raised that fret level. We always sold out of cinnamon rolls.

"So maybe we got hit with a double whammy this weekend," I said. "Roberta's scones and half-priced donuts."

"That's what I think. And I'm sure donuts up at the resort will cost a pretty penny at full price. People love half off anything."

I glanced at the leftover rolls. "Should I have a half off sale on these? But then it wouldn't be fair to the loyal customers who already came in and paid full price. Nope, I'm just going to deliver these to friends and call it a day."

"That sounds like a good idea. You need a relaxing afternoon. Well, I'm off to my fishing hole. Let's hope the fish are biting this morning."

"Good luck." My new plan had me eager to close up for the day. I needed a break. It had been a stressful few days. I divided the two dozen rolls, a mix of caramel pecan and cinnamon, into boxes to deliver to friends. I even made a box for Roberta to assure her I harbored no ill will toward her and that I wished her great luck and success with her teahouse.

The sun was out on a lovely, mild spring day. The earth was really starting to come alive again after a long, brittle winter. The new leaves on the aspen trees twittered like silver coins at the ends of brand-new stems. Bluebells, asters and butter cups had started their vast carpet of color in front yards and along the river, and annual migrators added splashes of color in the evergreens as they chirped and sang songs they seemed to reserve only for spring. I sneezed on my way across the road. Spring also meant pollen and hay fever, but it was easy to overlook the inconvenience in so much beauty.

Roxi's niece, Tanya, was behind the counter when I walked in. I remembered then that Roxi always took Sunday mornings off. Tanya had a beautiful smile with bright white teeth all perfectly aligned. "Hello, Scottie, how are you this morning?"

"Great, thanks. Is Roxi coming in later?" I placed my boxes on the table.

"Hmm, something smells delicious. Roxi was hoping to take the whole day off. She wanted to experiment with some new sandwich ideas."

I handed Tanya a box. "Then this is for you. You can take the leftovers home to Roxi. I made too many this morning."

Tanya opened the box. "Oh wow, these are exactly what my thighs don't need, but then again, thin thighs are overrated."

I laughed. "Couldn't agree more." I hated to admit that I couldn't find any fault with Tanya, and I was mad at myself for looking. I guess there was no way to deny that there was a sliver of jealousy involved after Nana insisted Tanya would be a good match for Dalton. After talking to him this morning, I realized that I wanted nothing more than for my old friend to be happy. He went through a lot of strife and turmoil with his engagement to Crystal, much like me and my engagement to Jonathan. Tanya might just be the perfect match for a man who was looking for a sweet and simple life with someone he adored. Crystal hadn't offered any of that. I wasn't sure he ever really liked her, let alone loved her. At least that was how I liked to remember their relationship. Crystal had always been a thorn in my side growing up and having her end up with the Dalton Braddock prize never sat right with me.

Tanya took a somewhat demure bite of the cinnamon roll and followed it by dabbing at her lip to get rid of the sticky bits left behind. So, there was one flaw—she was far too ladylike in her cinnamon roll consumption, but I was sure that could be overlooked.

"Well, I'm off to deliver my treats. Have a good day," I said.

"Oh, I will, especially with this to nibble on."

As I walked out of the market, I visualized her spending the rest of the day taking petite nibbles out of a cinnamon roll that was best savored in big, enthusiastic bites. Regina's gift shop next door was open. She rarely took time off, but she had such a nice homey set-up in the back room, with a sofa, a television and a kitchenette, that the shop was more like a second home. Like me, she only hired extra staff in the summer when visitors flooded her shop looking for Ripple Creek souvenirs.

The bell on the door rang as I pushed inside. There were boxes stacked along the walls, no doubt filled with T-shirts, hats and water bottles, ready to be put on shelves for the summer rush.

The bell brought Regina out from the back. I could smell bacon, and the television was on. "Scottie, it's you. How is Evie? Is she all right?" she asked frantically. I supposed her reaction was my fault. I rarely visited Regina in her store, even though she'd been a close friend of Nana's for years and her shop was just fifty feet away from mine. Some of that had to do with my lack of free time and some of it due to the fact that Regina was always a notorious gossip. Sometimes it was too much. Even Nana had to shut her down occasionally. Lately, it seemed she'd run dry of things to gossip about. We'd had a pretty quiet winter, and in those cold months, the locals tended to mostly hibernate inside.

"Nana's fine. She's feeling much better, thanks. I brought you a cinnamon roll and a caramel roll."

Her face lit up. "Well, aren't you sweet? You know how I love your baked goods." She didn't waste any time pulling a roll out of the box. "So, what do you think about Tanya, Roxi's niece? I hear there's a bit of a matchmaking scheme happening behind the scenes. Roxi and Evie think Dalton would be a good match for Tanya. What do you think about that?" Clearly, Regina was hoping for a significant reaction, one way or another, so she could relay my response to all who would care to listen. Unfortunately, it was not a secret in our small community that there had been something between Dalton and me. Of course, no one could define that *something* very well, but that didn't matter. It was enough to push some stories through the rumor mill.

I put on a pleasant, non-committal smile. "I think it's very nice," I said plainly. Regina shrank down in disappointment at my boring response.

"Well, I think they'd make a lovely couple." She was still fishing for a reaction.

"I'm sure they would. Well, enjoy your rolls. I've got a few more deliveries to make."

"Tell Evie I'll call her later to check on her. And thanks again for the treat, Scottie."

I hurried out. I liked Regina, and she was a good friend to Nana, but I could only take her in small sips.

sixteen

. . .

I WALKED across the street to my car. The day had started out so beautifully, fresh and green after yesterday's storm, that I almost rode my bike to work. The nip in the air was the only thing that kept me from rolling it out of the garage. Now that I was delivering cinnamon rolls, I was glad I'd opted for the car. I drove back through town and over the bridge to Cade's house. It was Sunday morning, but Cade generally worked every morning, even Sunday. He said his mind worked best in the early part of the day, then it got sluggish after lunch. That was usually the case with everyone. He also liked writing in the evening when the sun was down, and the only sounds around him were the ones nature provided. And there was plenty of that up on his vast, remote estate.

I pulled up to his house. He wasn't expecting me, but we'd also gotten to that level in our relationship where I had a key to his front door. I hadn't texted, so I knocked first and then entered.

"Is that you, Ramone? Or a stranger intent on chopping my head off with an ax?"

I laughed as I headed down the hallway to his office. "You, my friend, are spending far too much time writing gothic horror novels. I come bearing gifts." I held up the bakery box.

"Oh wow, I'm in need of such gifts this morning. Maybe a burst of blood sugar will get the words flowing." Like Regina and Tanya, Cade wasted no time pulling a plump, sticky roll from the box. He started with the caramel pecan, which I'd predicted. His laptop was open, and there was half a page of writing on the screen.

"I don't want to interrupt your work. I just wanted to deliver the treats."

"Hmm, needs milk." He motioned his head for me to follow him to the kitchen. "You aren't interrupting much. I'm using the delete button at top speed this morning."

We reached the kitchen.

"Why the treat delivery? Don't you usually sell out of these?"

"I do, but apparently I've got two evil opponents this weekend. Well, evil might be too strong of a word. 'Sugary opponents' works better. Roberta is still selling her scones at her yard sale, and there's a new donut shop up the hill that just opened. It's selling donuts at half price."

His eyebrow went up with great interest.

I put a hand on my hip. "Seriously? You've got a quarter-pound cinnamon roll sitting on your palm right now, and that roll was made with these loving hands." I held out both hands.

There was another brow lift, only this time it was cynical.

I nodded. "All right. They were made with Jack's loving hands, but you get my point."

Cade furrowed his brows. "Right," he said hesitantly. "Wait, is your point that I should be happy with the cinnamon roll and not even think about going up to get some half-off donuts?"

"Yes, that's it."

"Right," he said with an emphatic head nod. "That's what I thought. I wonder if they make buttermilk donuts? Those were always my favorite."

I sighed. "I will leave you to your traitorous donut thoughts." I hopped up and kissed him on the cheek. "Cinnamon Roll Santa has one more stop."

"Who?" he asked briskly, and I knew the reason for the sudden change in demeanor. He assumed I was taking one to Dalton, and frankly, I was a little miffed about his instant assumption.

"I'm taking some to Roberta to assure her I'm not the least bit worried about her opening a teahouse."

He nodded emphatically again. "Right. That's what I thought."

"No, it's not, but I'll forgive you. Now carry on. Hopefully the sugar rush will help."

I reached Roberta's house. The tables were all still out, though they contained considerably fewer items. I didn't see any customers ... or Roberta, for that matter. I got out of the car and walked toward the scone table. The sign was still up, and there were a half-dozen scones on a tray. The tub of clotted cream was mostly empty, but there was still enough for a few scones. The ice cream scoop she'd been using for the cream was sitting on the table. A trail of ants had found their way to the cream and to the jar of strawberry jam. Roberta had to have left the table unattended for an extended amount of time for the ants to move in unnoticed.

Harry came out of the house in a rush. His face was tight

with worry. "Scottie, have you seen Roberta? I can't find her anywhere. I was inside all morning watching soccer." He paused and looked down in shame. "I should have been out here helping her, but I didn't want to miss the game. And whenever I record a game, no fail, one of my buddies will text me asking if I saw such-and-such win the game, spoiling the whole thing." He was talking fast and nervously.

I put my hand on his shoulder. "Take a few deep breaths, Harry. You look close to a panic attack."

Harry took my advice, and the deep breaths helped.

"Now, tell me what's going on."

"Like I said, I was watching a game. There was a knock on the door. Peter and Violet, from down the street, were at the door holding a blender that Roberta was selling. They wanted to pay for it, and I was confused. I told them to pay Roberta, but they said they'd been waiting fifteen minutes, and they hadn't seen her. I finished the transaction and then walked out to the yard. There was no sign of Roberta. I thought maybe she'd gotten one of her bad headaches and that she decided to rest for a few minutes, but she wasn't in the bedroom ... or the bathroom ... or anywhere in the house. I checked the backyard. Her car is still in the garage, so she didn't go anywhere."

"Maybe she took a walk," I suggested, though it seemed strange to take one in the middle of her yard sale.

"Roberta suffers terrible problems with her feet. She never takes long walks." Harry rubbed his hands together. "What should I do?"

"Have you called her friends, her sister?"

His expression tightened. "Well, she's angered her friend, Mallory, so I'm sure she's not there. Besides, Mallory lives a few miles away, too far to go on Roberta's bad feet. And, well ..." he seemed hesitant to say the next part. "Janice and Roberta rarely speak. They're so different in many ways. They've never been close."

I agreed with that assessment, and I hardly knew them.

Harry felt around in his pockets for his phone. "Must have left my phone inside."

"I've brought you and Roberta some bakery treats. I'll carry them into the kitchen, and you and I can make some calls."

I followed Harry inside. A large screen television was paused right in the middle of a soccer game. The player's feet had left the ground to hit the ball with his head, and he was suspended midair on the screen. The kitchen was cluttered with mixing bowls, and there were two big soup-kettle-sized pots on the stove. A trash can was overflowing with empty cream cartons and butter wrappers.

I set down the box of rolls. Harry was on his phone. "Janice, it's me. Is Roberta with you, by any chance?" He nodded as if she could see him. "I don't know where she is, Janice. I'm worried." Harry looked beside himself. He nodded again. "Thanks. See you soon." He hung up. "Janice is coming over. She hasn't seen her."

"Well, maybe we'll have a big enough search team then to canvass the neighborhood. We can knock on doors to ask if anyone's seen her. Without a car and with problem feet, she can't have gone far. I'm sure she'll show up soon." I said it with conviction to calm his nerves, but my intuition and those darn ants outside were telling me something was terribly wrong.

seventeen
. . .

HARRY HAD WORKED himself into such a state of worry, I got him a glass of water and told him to sit down and rest. He was shaking and muttering something about how Roberta always pushed everyone too far, and most of the color had drained from his face. It seemed he was having the same dark, foreboding feeling as me. A grown woman doesn't just vanish into thin air, especially right from her front yard where she was busy with a yard sale.

Janice arrived just minutes after Harry called asking if she'd seen Roberta. She didn't look very worried until she saw the state that Harry was in. He looked up at her with a gaze that was almost feverish with concern. "So, you haven't seen her?" His voice shook as he asked the question.

Janice swept to his side and pulled up a chair. She placed her hand over his. "She'll show up, Harry. Don't worry. Scottie and I will talk to the neighbors. Surely someone has seen her."

Janice nodded at me to let me know we should start our

search. She was very calm, and I appreciated it. At the moment, Harry was better off staying inside and waiting. He didn't look well enough to go traipsing around the neighborhood.

We hadn't formalized a plan, but Janice pointed to the right. "I'll go that way, and you take the other side."

"Are there any neighbors that Roberta knows particularly well? Someone she might have coffee with occasionally or, at the very least, meet out on the sidewalk for a chat?" I asked. It seemed like a reasonable question, but Janice rolled her eyes.

"You really don't know my sister, do you? She was always so abrasive with people—she didn't make friends easily."

"Was?" I asked. "You said was."

She brushed it off. "Did I? I guess I'm more upset by this than I imagined." A fretful expression took over her face. "You don't think something's happened to her, do you? Surely, she just left the yard for a moment. I mean—look at this peaceful neighborhood." She waved her hand around. Her description was accurate. Neatly mowed lawns and tightly trimmed shrubs lined driveways leading up to quiet houses. The neighborhood oozed pride of ownership with its sweet mountain cottages and well-kept gardens. "I'm sure this whole mystery will end up with laughter and a round of hugs." She turned toward the neighbor's house, and I turned the opposite direction.

I walked up a stone path to a house with butter-yellow siding and a gray slate roof. Each window had a flower box filled with fake sunflowers. I knocked on the gray door and an elderly woman answered. It was Caroline Buxby. She used to take art lessons from Nana until the arthritis in her hands became too severe to hold a brush properly. Caroline must have been close to eighty, and she looked confused as she smiled hesitantly. It seemed she recognized me … but not entirely.

"Hi Caroline, it's me Scottie."

Her brows bunched in confusion, then I realized my mistake.

"I'm Evie's granddaughter." I was my own person, of course, but to many people in town, I was Evie's granddaughter before I was Scottie.

Her face lit up, and she leaned on her cane to look past me. "Is Evie with you?"

"No, she's at home. I'm sorry to bother you, Caroline—"

"Carol, please. Caroline is so formal. Would you like to come in for some coffee?" I felt bad having to turn her down. Something told me she didn't get too many visitors. Her husband, Bernard, had been gone at least ten years, and her only son moved out of state.

"Maybe some other time. In fact, I'll let Evie know, and we can make plans for a coffee visit."

That seemed to please her.

"Very well. See you then." She started to close the door, apparently thinking I'd shown up just to let her know I couldn't sit with her for coffee.

I placed my hand gently against the door to stop her from closing it. "Carol, I came by to see if you've seen Roberta Schubert this morning?"

The wrinkles in her forehead deepened. "Roberta?"

"Yes, your neighbor."

Her kind smile vanished. "Oh, her. She's having a noisy yard sale. You'll find her next door."

"Actually, I came here because she's not at her house. So, you haven't seen her?"

"Oh yes, I saw her," she said with an uncharacteristically harsh tone.

I perked up. "You saw her? Where did you see her?"

Caroline adjusted her cane to steady herself. "She was standing right there, on my stoop."

"Great. What time was that? Did you two talk?"

"Yes, we spoke. She walked over here to let me know that the windchimes hanging from the arbor in my yard were too noisy. She's always complaining about something, that one. But I haven't complained once about all her customers parking in front of my house or traipsing across my lawn."

I was anxious to get more information, but it wasn't easy. I needed to toss out one question at a time. "I'm sorry about that, Carol. What time did you see Roberta?"

Caroline lifted her hand to rub her chin in thought. Her knuckles protruded with arthritis, and her hand had a slight tremor. "Hmm, it's been such a long time now, but I remember Wendell, across the street, had just returned home with a Christmas tree on the top of his car, and there was snow on the ground."

I deflated quickly. Caroline had seen Roberta, just not this morning. "Right, I see. So, you haven't seen her *this* morning?"

"No, she'll be next door running her yard sale. Well, I'm getting quite tired standing here. Say hello to Evie for me."

"I will. Thank you for your help, Carol." I walked back down the stone path and glanced in the direction that Janice had walked. She was already four or five doors down. I'd just wasted precious time. I hurried to the next houses and found only a few people at home. No one had seen Roberta, and bringing up her name didn't exactly make people smile. Roberta seemed to be the neighborhood grouch.

Janice and I met back in Roberta's yard for a quick debriefing. "Oscar and Paula, who live next door, aren't home, and no one else has seen Roberta. I got the impression that very few people on this street even talk to my sister."

"I got the same feeling," I said. "And of the neighbors that were home, no one had seen her anywhere except right here at her yard sale."

Harry came out of the house wearing his heavy winter coat and still in full despair. "Have you found her?" he asked.

Janice leaned closer to me. "I'll take him back inside." She paused dramatically. "Maybe we should call Ranger Braddock."

I nodded. "I think so." I pulled out my phone to give Dalton a call.

"Hey, Scottie, everything all right? I'm just heading down from the resort."

I scoffed. "You went for the half-off donuts, didn't you?"

"Who? Me? Actually, I was called up there about a break-in, but afterward, a maple bar somehow magically appeared in my hand."

"Right. Almost believe that. I called for an important reason. I'm at Harry and Roberta Schubert's house. Roberta is missing."

"Missing? For how long?"

"Gosh, I don't know the specifics." I headed back up to the table where the dropped ice cream scoop was sitting in an ivory puddle of melted cream. There was now a solid line of ants moving back and forth between the jar of strawberry jam and their well-hidden ant farm destination. "According to the neighborhood ants, she left her scone table at least two hours ago, and I've got to say, Dalton, something doesn't feel right. She left abruptly. Harry hasn't seen her, and her sister and I canvassed the neighborhood. No one has seen her. Her car is in the garage."

"I'm sure she'll turn up but I'm on my way. Probably twenty minutes out."

"Twenty minutes and half a maple bar, I presume."

"Oh no, that beauty is long gone. See you soon."

Janice and I had gone straight to the neighbors, and I realized I hadn't really looked around Roberta's own yard. The tables had been made neater this morning. They'd been in quite the state of disarray yesterday after the flurry of customers, so at some point in time, possibly even last night, Roberta straightened up her merchandise to get ready for another day.

I circled around each table, not entirely sure what I was looking for. It wasn't until I reached the far side of the yard, the side that bordered Oscar and Paula's property, that I noticed something interesting. The two yards were separated by several rows of pink phlox, newly planted based on the freshly turned soil. A cluster of the plants had been flattened as if someone had marched through them. Certainly, something had ruined the delicate buds, and if it had been a deer, it would have nibbled the petals off before trampling the plants. I would also expect to see some hoof prints in the fresh soil. The loose dirt looked as if it had been stomped across, not hopped across by hooves.

There was more fresh soil on Oscar's cement driveway, and a few smudges of it led to the side gate. It was very scant, and I was probably just chasing down the path of a rabbit or squirrel, but I decided to walk through the gate. Dalton would arrive soon, and he'd understand why I walked into the backyard uninvited. At least, I was pretty sure he would.

The yard was mostly gray pavers and neatly trimmed lawn. Two wicker chairs with brightly colored pillows sat under a patio awning. The yard was surrounded by a wooden privacy fence. A garden shed sat in the far corner of the yard. I looked at the shed and that grim feeling that had been with me since Harry told me Roberta was missing gripped me tightly.

I walked cautiously toward the shed. The door was slightly ajar, an inch at most. The gray pavers ended about three feet from the shed, and the path continued with pea gravel. There were two marks where the gravel had been moved aside as if someone had dragged something heavy across it. My intuition really kicked in, and my heart raced. I yanked my shirt sleeve down to cover my hand and reached for the handle. I pulled open the chunky plastic door and found exactly what I expected—Roberta Schubert, dead on the floor of the shed. Her eyes and mouth were wide open. A thin piece of rope was draped loosely around her neck.

eighteen

. . .

STILL COVERING my hand with my shirt, I cautiously closed the shed and walked back across to Roberta's yard. I was relieved to see that Harry and Janice were still inside the house. I certainly didn't want to be the one to tell them the horrible news. That unenviable job fell to Dalton.

I stayed out of view of the front window and pulled out my phone.

"Five minutes away," Dalton said before I could speak.

"That's good because Roberta is dead. And it wasn't natural causes. There's a rope around her neck." I was being blunt, but I wasn't sure how else to relay the news.

There was a long pause on his side. "Darn," he said. "Well, I'll be there in a few. How is Harry taking it?"

"He's still inside, and well, you're the official. It'll be better coming from you."

Another pause. "Worst part of the job. See you soon."

Minutes later, Dalton's truck pulled up to the curb out front. Janice immediately came outside. Harry stayed in the doorway, still looking as if he might collapse from worry. Soon, that worry would turn to grief.

"Thank goodness, you're here, Ranger Braddock," Janice said. "We're just beside ourselves. Where on earth could she be?"

Dalton shifted a secretive glance my direction. I shrugged discreetly in response. Dalton held up a finger to stop Janice. "I'm going to take a look around first." I knew he wanted to confirm that Roberta was, indeed, dead. It wasn't the kind of news you broke to family without being confident. "Why don't you take Harry back inside?" Dalton suggested. "He looks pale."

Janice nodded in agreement. "Poor man is so distraught. I do hope your arrival will give us some answers." She returned to the house and easily talked a frail, shaky Harry back inside.

I motioned for Dalton to follow me across to Oscar's yard. "Is the owner home?" he asked.

"No one's home." I reached for the gate, but Dalton stopped me and pulled on a glove.

I winced. "Oops, I touched the gate earlier. In my defense, I had no idea I'd find her back here. I did, however, feel that I was about to come upon a grisly scene when I walked to that shed. I pulled my shirt down to cover my hand." I demonstrated. "Never touched the doorknob with a bare hand."

"Well done." Dalton took a deep, steadying breath and opened the door. He stood there for a long moment staring down at the body. "Guess there's no mistaking this for anything but murder. I'm going to need to call the coroner, then I'll go back to the house and deliver the news." Another steadying breath. "Sure wasn't expecting this today."

While Dalton performed all the official duties that came with his job, I walked one more house over to Oscar's other neighbor. Maybe they'd heard or seen something. I knocked and two kids answered the door. They looked to be around ten or eleven. I didn't recognize them, but the woman who came to the door after them was Darla Lincoln. The two children must have been her visiting grandkids. She tapped each playfully on the head. "Go clean up your toys. Your dad will be here soon."

"Scottie," Darla said looking a little stunned. "Have they still not found Roberta? Or are you here for a different reason?"

"No, I'm here about Roberta." It certainly wasn't my place to spread the news of her death, so I kept that to myself. "Uh, by any chance, did you hear or see anything unusual next door at Oscar and Paula's house? It looks as if someone has been in their yard. They're not home right now."

"No, they drove down to the city to pick up a new couch. But now that you mention it—I did hear Rex, their dog, barking. He's inside the house, but he's usually pretty quiet."

"What time was that?"

"Let me see, I was fixing lunch for the kids, so it must have been around eleven. I didn't look out the window, but I heard Rex barking. I figured Oscar was getting a delivery or something." Darla's face pinched. "Did something happen? What's going on? Is Roberta all right?"

"Well, Ranger Braddock is here now, so we'll know more soon. I'll pass on the information about Rex barking."

I cut back through Oscar's yard. A spring breeze ruffled the trees and even though it was a tender, nice breeze, I knew it was whispering the possibility of an afternoon thunderstorm. The few scant bits of evidence I'd noticed would be washed away. I walked back to the shed and took photos of the disturbance in the pea gravel and then finished with some pictures of the scattered dirt on both the driveway and near the phlox plants. I got a few good shots of the destroyed flowers before heading toward Harry's house.

Harry's front door opened, and Janice walked out. She was hunched over and had a tissue pressed to her nose. She walked down the steps cautiously, and once she reached yard level, she hurried across to me. "Oh, my goodness, Scottie, did you hear?" She blew her nose. Her eyes were puffy. "Ranger Braddock says Roberta is dead. He hasn't given us details. Do you know anything?"

I hated to lie to a bereaved sister, but I shook my head. "We'll have to wait for Ranger Braddock to fill us in. I'm very sorry, Janice. When was the last time you spoke to your sister?"

"Yesterday at the yard sale. That's right. You were there. I still can't believe she's gone. My only sibling." She dropped her face into her hands, and I put my arm around her shoulders.

The coroner van's arrival was always an ominous sight to see, but it looked especially out of place in the serene, cozy neighborhood. Soon everyone would wander out of their houses to find out what was happening at the Schubert residence. And since Janice and I had talked to many of them, they'd know the official vehicles had something to do with Roberta's disappearance.

"Oh dear, oh dear," Janice said when she saw the van. "I'm so glad my parents aren't alive. This would have destroyed them. I'm all alone now," she said sadly.

The front door opened, and Dalton walked out.

"I'd better get back inside," Janice said. "Poor Harry is in utter despair." She left me and placed her hand on Dalton's arm as he passed her. He patted her hand and then continued toward the coroner's team.

"I've got a few photos of ruffled dirt and broken plants. And you might want to speak to the neighbor, Darla, on the other side of Oscar's house. She heard Oscar's dog barking around eleven. I'm going to head home and check on Nana. Keep me posted."

nineteen

. . .

I TUCKED A BLANKET AROUND NANA. She'd fallen asleep in the big chair shortly after I got home. The afternoon sunlight was weak, made even less effective by the trees around the cottage, so the house felt chilly. I planned to make delicious lentil soup and fresh rolls for a quiet weekend dinner.

The first half of the day had been far too eventful and explosive for my liking. Sunday afternoon was usually the start of my already too short weekend, but I couldn't unwind. After months of peace and quiet, the town had been, once again, rocked by a murder. And it was extra shocking that it was a longtime resident, a person who everyone knew well. Roberta was not the most beloved person in town, but people would be talking about this for months. Of course, I was dying to see what evidence Dalton and the coroner's team found at the murder scene, but since I'd chosen to be with Cade instead of Dalton, he found more reasons to keep me from nosing around in his cases.

Nana stirred and worked hard to open her eyes. "Button?"

she said weakly. "How long have I been sleeping?" She sat up straighter and without thinking reached up to wipe her eyes, but her left eye was met with a heavy swath of bandages. It startled her awake more. "Oh, this darn thing." She sniffed the air. "No dinner yet?"

"It's still a few hours off, but I'm going to chop vegetables right now to get a head start."

"I slept so heavily." Nana looked up at me, confused. "Did Roberta Schubert die, or did I dream that?"

"Not a dream. She's dead. I was telling you all about it before you started a hurricane of yawns and then you drifted off."

Nana shook her head and pushed forward on the chair. "It's this darn chair. It's too comfortable, and I'm not sleeping as well at night. It's hard to move around without the use of both arms. Getting comfortable takes time. And these long afternoon naps aren't helping. I'm usually so busy all day that I'm ready to fall fast asleep at night, but I'm just a useless couch potato right now."

I leaned down and kissed her forehead. "You're not useless, and you're certainly not a couch potato."

"No, but I'm a big, easy-chair potato. Which reminds me, there's half a bag of small yellow potatoes in the pantry for the soup. They need to be used soon before they go bad. Should I help?"

"You can come sit in the kitchen and keep me company while I cut veggies. Do you want some coffee?" I offered her my hand to help her out of the deep chair.

"No, it's far too late in the day for coffee, but I wouldn't mind a glass of orange juice. That nap has sapped me of energy."

"Orange juice coming right up."

Nana settled at the table with her juice, and I told her a few of the details about Roberta's death as I cut onions, carrots, celery and potatoes for Nana's much-loved lentil soup recipe. I pulled out the soup pot, rinsed lentils and prepared the spice mix to be added once the veggies were cooking. A knock on the door yanked us from our casual conversation.

"I wonder who that could be." Nana moved to get up.

I put up a hand. "No, I'll get it. It's probably Hannah."

Nana laughed as I walked out of the kitchen because Hannah rarely knocked. I could see Dalton's ranger truck parked in front of the house as I headed to the door.

I opened the door, enthusiastically, certain he'd decided to stop by and fill me in on pertinent details of the case. He wore what I considered to be a grave expression. "Dalton? What's up?"

"Can I come in?" he asked.

"Of course."

I could hear him taking a deep breath as he stepped past me.

"Has something happened? Is there another body?"

Nana heard Dalton's voice, and she came out of the kitchen. I got the sense that Dalton wished she'd stayed away.

He was holding his hat in his hands, spinning it nervously in his fingers. He took another deep breath. "Well, there's no easy way to say this, except I want to preface it with the phrase 'I'm just doing my job.'"

"What on earth is going on?" I asked.

"Scottie Ramone, I need to take you down to the station for questioning in the death of Roberta Schubert."

I stood as still as a statue and waited for him to break the serious façade and laugh. Instead, he kept his gaze averted, not able to look Nana or me in the eye.

Nana was the first to speak. "Dalton, you can't be serious. Obviously, Scottie had nothing to do with it."

"I'm sure that's the case," Dalton said.

A dry, nervous laugh shot from my mouth. "You're sure? You didn't say that with even an ounce of sureness."

Now that the initial announcement was over, Dalton found the courage to look at me. "I'm sorry, Scottie, but we found a napkin from your bakery underneath Roberta's body, and you were the person to find her."

"Yes, because I was out there actively looking for her and because my skills at finding evidence and noticing when something seems out of place are so finely honed it helped me locate her body. What motive could I possibly have? Oh wait, don't tell me. Roberta's teahouse plan might hurt my business?"

He didn't answer but then he didn't have to. I stuck my hands out. "Go ahead, cuff me."

Dalton rolled his eyes. "It's not an arrest. I'm just bringing you in for questioning. Again, Scottie, I'm just doing my job."

"Fine, can I drive over on my own? I'm making soup for Nana, and I want to hurry back."

Dalton nodded. He still hadn't looked in Nana's direction. "I'm sorry about all this," he muttered and hurried out the door.

I looked at Nana and she shrugged.

"He's just doing his job," she said dryly.

"I guess so." I grabbed my purse and keys. "I'll be back soon … I hope."

I walked into the station without looking at Dalton. He turned and I followed him to a room in the back. There was a long, metal table sitting between two chairs. The room was painted gray, and it gave off all gray vibes. I finally looked at him with a "seriously?" expression.

"Like I said—" he started.

"Doing your job. Yep. You've mentioned that." I sat down on the chair with an angry, defiant plunk. "Alibis," I said before he could fire off his first question. "I've got them. Roberta died around eleven. No doubt that was when the *actual* killer was strangling Roberta. I closed my bakery at half-past ten, then I walked across the street to the market. Tanya was there alone for the morning. She ate the cinnamon roll I brought, and we talked, then I walked next door to Regina's shop. I was there for about five minutes, then I drove over to Cade's house. From there I drove to Roberta's house. Got there about noon. Harry was already upset because he couldn't find Roberta. I jumped into immediate action to help."

Dalton started writing names down on a pad of paper. "So, you saw Regina, Tanya and Cade between the time you left the bakery and the time you arrived at Roberta's house?"

"Yes." We were speaking like two strangers, and it left me with a cold knot in my stomach. I hoped he was feeling that same cold knot, because he deserved it. "Why did I need to come in for this?" I asked in a wavering tone. Now my anger was cracking and beneath it was a big layer of hurt.

"I told you, Scottie, they found one of your bakery napkins under Roberta's body, and you were at the scene and you found the body. I know it wasn't you, but how would it look if I ignored all that and the possible motive because we were friends? I have to go by the book on this. Bringing you in shows that I'm serious about this investigation. The coroner's team found the napkin and bagged it for evidence."

"Fine, I suppose that works as an explanation, but I'm still upset."

"I know. I'm sorry. I'll talk to Tanya and Regina to corroborate your alibi, and that will be the end of it."

"And Cade," I reminded him.

His jaw tightened. "The two women should be enough." Cade and Dalton avoided each other like a plague and even more so now that Cade and I were together.

I smiled. "Darn, and I really would have liked to hear how that conversation went." I shouldn't have pushed my luck. We'd finally broken through the stranger façade, and now he was wearing that official expression again. "I'll let you know if I need more information from you," he said plainly.

"All right, I'm sorry. I shouldn't have teased about you talking to Cade. But now that we're sitting in a very secure room with no one around to hear—what else did they find? Other than the napkin—a napkin that is probably wadded up in every coat pocket in town, by the way."

"I know that, of course. What do you think I use to wipe the haze off my cold windshield in the morning?"

"Well, I'm glad my napkins have a dual purpose, but don't you ever leave behind—"

"Crumbs on my windshield? Yes. One day I ended up smearing glaze on the glass. Look, about the case, you know I can't talk to you about it. Especially this time since—"

I sat up straighter. "Since I'm a suspect?"

"Well, technically, yes."

"Great. I hope you find the killer soon. Am I free to go? Nana's expecting lentil soup."

Dalton's eyes rounded. "Her famous recipe?"

"Yes. I'm making it, but she'll be there to coach me through it. Too bad we're at this new, rather strained juncture in our friendship. Otherwise, I'd invite you over for a bowl, but I think we better keep things professional—you know—cuz that's your job."

Dalton blew out an exasperated puff of air as he opened the door. I stopped in the doorway and looked back at the bleak room. "Always wondered what it looked like in here. I personally think it needs a little color. Goodbye, Ranger Braddock."

He nodded. "Miss Ramone."

twenty

. . .

IT WOULDN'T TAKE LONG to put the soup together, so I decided to make a quick pit stop. Since I was a suspect in this murder case, I decided it was more important than ever to do some investigating of my own. I'd mentioned a few small details to Dalton while we were at the site and before I became a suspect. There were the broken plants, the loose dirt leading to Oscar's gate and Darla's mention of the dog barking, but I'd witnessed several altercations between Roberta and people at the yard sale. Dalton knew Mallory was upset about her teapot, but apparently since there was a bakery napkin at the scene, Mallory wasn't on his list. He wouldn't share anything else he'd learned. At the same time, he never asked me if I had anything else to add. Boy, did I. I just didn't feel the need to share it voluntarily. I was going to find the killer without his official help.

The Schuberts used to live in the house that they were currently renting to Arnie Morris. Arnie had shown up at the yard sale with an eviction notice bunched in his fist, and he was plenty mad about it. Apparently, after a big rent increase didn't push Arnie out of the rental, Roberta took further action and sent him an eviction notice. She'd planned to get the place ready to put on the market. The sale of their old house was going to help finance her teahouse.

Roberta all but laughed him off the property, and Arnie left filled with rage. It was a stretch to think that he came back the next morning to kill Roberta, but the man had motive. The rental house was a few blocks away from the house they'd inherited from Eleanor. The neighborhood was mostly rentals, and so "pride of ownership" was not as evident. The yards weren't filled with flowers, and some of the lawns had been replaced with easier to manage gravel. Roberta's rental looked even shabbier than the rest. It badly needed a coat of paint, and the yard was just gravel and weeds. Someone had slapped a coat of blue paint on the front door, but they hadn't taken the time to sand and prime first, so the old red paint showed through.

Music was playing somewhere in the house, so I knocked firmly. Arnie came to the door. He was wearing an old Rolling Stones T-shirt, shorts and no shoes. He looked more than surprised to see me.

"Scottie?"

"Yes, hello." I looked past him and noticed several big boxes sitting in the middle of the front room. "You're moving," I said.

"That's right. Where are my manners? Come on in, but you'll have to excuse the chaos. I've started a throwaway pile." He pointed to a cluster of items, clothes, shoes, artwork and even a small table. "But then, I walk by it and think 'wait, maybe I won't get rid of that.' I've been living here for five years, so I've accumulated a lot of stuff."

"Trust me—I know how that works." It occurred to me right then, alarmingly for the first time, that Arnie might not have heard the news. "Excuse me for mentioning it—but I was at the yard sale yesterday, and you arrived very upset, and rightly so, about the eviction notice Roberta sent you."

"Yeah, that old crow, she's a tough bird. I decided it wasn't worth fighting her over it. Admittedly, I came home after that scene and marched to the phone to call my lawyer. It didn't seem fair, but then I looked around at this place." He paused to glance around the room. Past the mountain of boxes, the walls were stained and a dingy white. The carpeting was so worn out, you could see the padding showing through and a mildew smell seemed to permeate the whole house. "I decided—why am I putting up such a fuss to stay in this dump? I've sent Roberta a long list of repairs, and she's never fixed anything. Wait till she finds out how much money she's going to need to spend to make this place sellable. I went right down to the hardware store and bought boxes, and I've been having a good laugh as I pack up my things. I'm going to put my stuff in storage and then stay with a friend for a month or so. It's always nice to get a new perspective and fresh surroundings."

That was it, my cue that Arnie still hadn't heard about Roberta. "Uh, Arnie, I guess you haven't heard the news."

Arnie got distracted by a pair of shoes that were sitting in the throwaway pile. He held up his hand to stop me and grabbed the shoes out of the pile. "You never know when you'll need an extra pair of shoes." He dropped them into another pile, which I assumed were the "keepers."

"Now, what news is that?"

"Not sure how to tell you this, so I guess I'll just say it. Roberta Schubert is dead."

He stared at me with this faint, odd smile. "Dead? As in not living?"

"Pretty much the only dead I know about."

"What happened?" Arnie reached blindly back for the arm of the couch. It took him a second to find it before sitting down. That was when I noticed some scratches on his arm. Suddenly, I had a vision of Roberta clutching her attacker's arms in an attempt to get free of his grasp. Maybe the innocent, "gee, what news?" was an act.

It wasn't my place to give out details, and if Dalton was somehow led to Arnie to question him, he'd never forgive me if I messed up his investigation by handing out specifics. "I'm not entirely sure."

"But she's dead? You know for certain that she's dead?" He asked it with a touch too much enthusiasm.

"She's dead," I repeated.

Arnie rubbed his hand through his short hair. "Gosh, that's a shocker. Poor Harry. I always liked him better than his wife. He's a good guy."

"That's right. Harry took you into the house to talk, but when you marched out you still looked rather upset." That was putting it mildly.

"I thought I'd gotten through to Harry at first. You know, he's such a kind, polite guy, and it seemed he was siding with me. He told me he didn't think Roberta would even go through with any of her plans. When I asked him if he could speak to her about letting me stay, he practically shuddered at the thought. He was afraid of Roberta. She ruled the roost, as they say. He told me it was Roberta's decision because she was in charge of the finances. So, I turned hard on my heels and left. I had to bite my tongue not to call him a coward. I was so angry." He paused. "Did someone hurt Roberta?"

"I'm not entirely sure how she died. When was the last time you saw her?"

"Me? Yesterday at the yard sale." His eyes squinted slightly in suspicion but I pressed on.

I looked pointedly at his arm. "Do you have a cat?"

He glanced at the cuts. "No, I was trying to cut some of the overgrown roses in the backyard. I guess I needed longer gloves." He tilted his head with a questioning look. "You never told me why you're here." His brow furrowed, and some of that anger I'd seen the day before crept back into his expression.

"I was driving past, and I thought I'd check in on you. You looked so upset yesterday. I was going to mention that I saw a 'for rent' sign on a cabin a few miles up the highway." I considered it an admirable save, and he seemed to buy it, but it seemed I was overstaying my welcome.

"Right. Well, that was kind of you, and I'll drive up the highway to check out the cabin."

"I've got to get home and make dinner for my grandmother." I walked to the door and he followed.

"Be sure to tell her hello for me," he said and then snapped the door shut rather sharply behind me.

twenty-one

. . .

MY VISIT with Arnie left me feeling undecided. He was packing, so it seemed he'd made up his mind to vacate the rental. In fact, he even had a plan of where he'd live for the next month while his things stayed in storage. If he was already resolved to move out, he had no motive to kill Roberta. He didn't care for her, but then Roberta was not exactly a beloved town member. The scratches on his arms were suspicious, however, he quickly had a reasonable explanation that he'd been trimming roses. His explanation seemed slightly implausible given the general state of the house and yard. Why bother trimming rosebushes when the entire yard was a mass of weeds? I considered looking around the back to check for the existence of rosebushes, but after Arnie had snapped the door shut, I decided to give that leg of my investigation a rest.

Nana was reading a book and looked decidedly bored as I walked in. Normally, on a Sunday afternoon, weather permitting, she and Hannah would take a walk around the neighborhood. In spring, she'd carry a small notebook to write down the birds and nests she spotted on the walk. She liked to keep track of the migrators and their fledglings. Then she'd come home and start dinner.

Nana sat forward and twisted from side to side to ease the ache in her back. She was not used to sitting for such long periods of time. "How did it go with Dalton?" she asked as if we'd just gone out for coffee. "Obviously, he knows you didn't kill Roberta." A soft chuckle followed.

"I'm not so sure about that. But for now, I'm a free woman," I said lightly. I was feeling the sting of Dalton's accusation much more than my grandmother.

"I'm sure it'll be cleared up soon. You can't blame Dalton. He's just doing his job."

"Yes, so I've been told. It'd be nice to know that my grandmother was more on my side than his."

Nana pushed off from the couch. Having only one arm to help her made it a bit of a struggle. "Oh, come now, Button. Of course, I'm always on your side, just like I know you didn't kill anyone."

"I'm glad to hear that."

Nana reached back with her good hand and rubbed her neck. "Sitting so much is turning me into a proper old lady with creaky bones and muscles that no longer work."

"Nana, it occurs to me that you could still take a walk with Hannah. Just be careful, maybe take along your walking stick. Your balance might be off some because of your broken wing." I moved my elbow up and down to demonstrate a wing.

Nana stifled a yawn. "You know, Button, maybe you're right. I've got two working legs. I'll give Hannah a call and see if she'd like to take a short turn around the neighborhood."

"I think that's a great idea. I'm going to put the soup on and then if you could just keep an eye on it while it's cooking, I've got a quick errand to run."

The yard sale had given me a small, almost intimate glimpse into Roberta's life. I hadn't realized until her murder that she was a rather ruthless and, by the looks of it, lazy landlord, and she was the culprit behind Mallory's missing teapot debacle. I was probably in Paris training to be a pastry chef when the teapot went mysteriously missing, but it seemed that Mallory just about had the whole town looking for it.

"Sure, I can watch the soup. I'm done sitting here on this lumpy couch acting as if I can't move. It's depressing."

"Well, don't go too crazy. A short walk and give the soup a few stirs."

"I guess I'll leave my roller skates at home then," Nana said with a teasing smile. "What errand do you have to run?"

I never kept anything from Nana. I'd called it an errand out of lack of a better term. "I'm going to see Mallory Cook."

"Mallory?" It took Nana a second to remember the teapot fiasco. "Oh, right, Mallory. Why would you be visiting Mallory? Do you think she had something to do with Roberta's death?"

"Let's just say she's a person of interest." Nana had an infallible historical record of Ripple Creek stored up in that amazing brain of hers. "Nana, do you remember anything else about Mallory's missing heirloom teapot? I know it happened ten years ago, but any little detail might help."

Nana was already nodding. "Yes, she was so distraught, and we all had a photocopied picture of the teapot under magnets on our fridges. That way, if we spotted it somewhere—a yard sale or an antique shop—we could let Mallory know. It was as if the thing just vanished into thin air."

"Until now," I said.

Nana's mouth dropped open. "I still can't believe Roberta did that to her friend."

"Roberta had very casually put it out at her yard sale. She either forgot she stole it, or she didn't consider the possibility of Mallory showing up at the yard sale. It was quite the scene yesterday. I thought I'd pay Mallory a visit. You should go on that walk before it gets dark. And take your walking stick."

I'd pre-cut all the soup ingredients, so it didn't take long to put the soup together. I left it to simmer on the stove. Nana was just returning from her walk as I stepped out the door. The sun was setting and leaving behind a brisk breeze. Nana's cheeks were rosy, and she was smiling. The walk had done her a world of good.

"You look so much better." I gave her a hug.

"I feel much better. Thank you, Button, for suggesting it. I guess I was treating myself like a fragile teacup because of a broken wrist. I'll keep an eye on the soup. Don't be long."

"I won't be. See you soon."

Mallory Cook's house wore a touch of her eccentric style. The house was yellow, and the shutters were lavender. There was a metal sculpture in the front yard that I couldn't quite make out, but I was sure somewhere within the mash of metal was a pelican. Mallory had never married. When I was in school, she worked in the high school office as a clerk. Unlike the school secretary, Mrs. Horsham, who'd look you up and down with suspicion if you dared walk into the office, Mallory was always friendly and helpful.

I could hear the television running as I knocked. Mallory came to the door wearing a leopard-print sweatsuit. Her black hair was bundled up on her head, exposing a long row of gray roots beneath. "Scottie, what a surprise."

"Hi, Mallory, I came to check on you. I was at the yard sale on Saturday when you found your great-grandmother's teapot. And I know you spoke to Dalton about it this morning. I'm sorry there wasn't more he could do."

"Thank you, Scottie, and the cinnamon roll was delicious. After the yard sale, I was in such a state—as I'm sure you can imagine—I'm sorry we didn't get a chance to talk." Her face twisted in concern. "Now—I've heard something from my neighbor, Mary, only she's the type who runs off with a story and turns it completely upside down. She told me something quite alarming, so alarming I'm not inclined to believe it, but I know nothing gets past your grandmother, and so maybe you can confirm or deny. Mary said that Roberta Schubert was dead —a heart attack or some sort of accident—she presumed."

At least this time I didn't have to break the shocking news. Not that I was entirely sure Arnie hadn't already been *very* aware of Roberta's death. He was still on my suspect list. "It's true that Roberta is dead. I don't know many details. Did you happen to see her today? I thought you might have gone back to talk to her again after discovering that she'd had your teapot all along."

Mallory's mouth pursed up as if she'd sucked on a lemon. It seemed she was contemplating whether or not to tell me something.

"That's all right. I don't mean to pry. It's just you looked so shocked by your discovery of the teapot."

Mallory blew out an exasperated breath. She looked across the room and that was when I spotted the teapot. It was sitting on a shelf between some silver candlesticks. "I was beyond shocked, if there's a word for that. I almost pinched myself just to make sure I wasn't having a weird, bad dream. I can't even tell you how I felt when I realized that my own friend had betrayed me. Roberta had been part of my inner circle of friends, and she put out flyers everywhere looking for the teapot. And, all that time, her concern was fake. She had the pot all along and then she barely said one word about it when I confronted her. She tried to tell me I was mistaken as if I wouldn't recognize my own family heirloom. It's truly one of a kind."

"I'm glad you have it back now."

"You know, I did go to Roberta's this morning," she blurted as if it had weighed heavily on her mind, and now she'd relieved herself of the burden.

I tried not to show extreme interest. I didn't want to scare her off or rouse suspicion about the real reason for my visit. "Oh, did you?" I asked lightly.

"I did. I couldn't sleep all night, tossing and turning over what I considered to be the ultimate betrayal by a friend. I wanted her arrested, but since that wasn't going to happen, I thought I might confront her and let her know just how vile a person she was."

"How did that conversation go?" I asked.

"It didn't. Roberta wasn't at the yard sale. There was no sign of her. She'd even left her scones out on the table unattended. I knocked on the front door, but there was a game of some sort, football or soccer, blasting on the television, so no one heard me. By then, I'd lost the fire in my belly, so to speak. I had my teapot, and I was just as happy to never see or speak to Roberta again. I got back in the car and left."

"What time was that?"

"Gosh, I guess around eleven." It was one question too far.

Mallory squinted at me. "What's going on? It wasn't a heart attack, was it?"

"I can't tell you details, but no, it wasn't a heart attack."

"Oh my, well, that puts a different spin on it. All I can say is Roberta had a lot of—I don't know if you'd call them enemies—but people didn't like her. She was abrasive and rude and frankly, I'm still asking myself why I had anything to do with her in the first place. I'm pretty convinced that she took that teapot just to upset me. It's an heirloom with mostly sentimental value. It wouldn't fetch more than a few hundred dollars at an antique auction, and only if the right buyer showed up. And I don't think it was her style either. She just did it to upset me. Not a great friend."

"Definitely not a great friend. I won't take up any more of your time, Mallory. I'm glad the teapot is right where it belongs."

"Let me know if you hear anything else about Roberta's death. I didn't like her anymore, but it's a shame that she's dead. I'm sure Harry is beside himself."

"Yes, he's very grief-stricken." I waved goodbye and headed out to the car. That was the end of today's investigation, and I was feeling pretty underwhelmed by my progress so far.

twenty-two
. . .

IT HAD BEEN QUITE the day. It started with a disappointing lack of customers for my Sunday morning specials. Of course, that was nothing compared to the shock of arriving at Roberta's and eventually finding her murdered in a neighbor's backyard shed. Dalton showing up at the door to take me in for questioning had put a nice, sour cherry on top for the finale, but the day wasn't over yet.

I was surprised to see Dalton's truck sitting out front of Nana's house when I came around the corner. Another car, a silver sedan, was parked in front of the truck. Had Dalton come back to make my arrest final? I was nervous walking up to the house. Had he found more evidence? I'd told him about touching the gate on my way into Oscar's yard. Were my prints now part of the evidence collection? I should never have gotten involved, and it had all started with the innocent, peace-keeping gesture of delivering Roberta free cinnamon rolls.

I opened the door and immediately was hit with both the

spicy aroma of the soup and laughter, familiar and unfamiliar. Nana was in the kitchen with her guests.

I put down my things. "Scottie, is that you?" Nana called. "Come say hello."

It seemed my grandmother really was the forgiving sort. She'd not only pushed aside the earlier scene where Dalton all but accused me of murder, but she'd even taken pains to invite him to dinner … to eat the soup I cooked. But that wasn't the big stunner of the evening. As I entered the kitchen, I discovered that Tanya was the second guest at the table.

She smiled up at me as she sat behind a bowl of steamy soup. "Hello, Scottie. That's twice in one day. Scottie brought me the most delicious bakery treats this morning," she explained.

Nana smiled up at me next, and there was a devilish twinkle in her eye because she knew she'd done something that would probably not sit well with me. "Serve yourself a bowl, Button. It's delicious. Almost as good as mine."

"I'm so glad it passes muster," I said with heavy sarcasm. I was no longer hungry, but I didn't want to be rude. I ladled myself a bowl of soup and sat down next to Nana. Dalton was going out of his way to avoid eye contact, but I stared straight at him to let him know I was still miffed about this afternoon.

"How was Mallory?" Nana asked.

The mention of her name finally made Dalton turn my direction. "Mallory Cook?" he asked.

I lifted my chin confidently. "Yes, I stopped by to have a little chat with her."

"I still can't believe that Roberta had that teapot all this time," Nana said. I usually adored everything about my grandmother, but this evening she was stepping on more than one nerve.

"How much do you know about the teapot incident?" Dalton asked.

"I saw the whole thing unfold right before my eyes," I said.

Dalton forced a smile at Tanya and Nana. "If you'll excuse us for a second, I need to talk to Scottie." He stood up and motioned for me to follow him out.

I was mid-bite from my soup. I finished the bite, took a sip of water and then carefully blotted my mouth with my napkin. His jaw grew tight with impatience.

I got up and followed him outside to the front stoop. "You're doing a shadow investigation. I've asked you to stay away from this case, Scottie."

"Well, it seems I have a much larger stake in this case than usual. Or did you forget that you hauled me into the station?"

"I didn't forget, and something tells me I'll never forget because you'll constantly remind me about it. You witnessed the two women arguing? How bad was it?"

"It was pretty heated, but since you were focused on me as a suspect—"

"I could charge you with obstructing justice."

I stared straight at him. "For what? For attending a yard sale and witnessing an argument between two friends?"

"Two friends and one of them just happened to be strangled to death this morning."

Now I perked up. "So, it was definitely strangulation?"

He shook his head. "You know it was. You saw the rope around her neck."

"But was there a struggle?" I asked. I was still thinking about the scratches on Arnie's arm. I supposed it would only be right for me to bring up Arnie's visit as well, but I decided I'd only do that if he brought it up first.

"It seemed she did try to fight off her attacker."

"Was she killed in the shed or dragged there?"

Dalton raised a brow at me. "How did you turn this around so quickly? You're supposed to be telling me what you know. Not the other way around. What did Mallory say? I'm going to speak to her in the morning."

"She just said she was shocked that her friend, Roberta, had betrayed her so badly. She said she went to speak with her this morning, but Roberta wasn't there."

"Right, well, stay out of this case." He looked at me and rolled his eyes. "I'm just wasting my breath."

"We should get back in before the soup gets cold," I said. "And uh, you are aware of my grandmother's matchmaking plot, right?"

"I'm a willing participant," he said curtly.

"Oh, well, then—good for you." I hated that it irritated me. I should have been happy for him, but I wasn't feeling all that charitable toward Dalton Braddock at the moment.

twenty-three
. . .

I MIGHT HAVE BEEN USING a touch too much *energy* washing the dishes. I managed to crack a soup bowl as I lifted it from the soapy water and smacked it on the faucet. Nana was in the front room, but she heard it.

"What on earth did those soup bowls ever do to you, Button?"

"Sorry," I called back.

A moment later, her stockinged feet tapped the floor behind me. "You're mad," she said.

"No, not at all. One moment, Dalton is threatening to jail me for murder, and the next, my grandmother, the person who is nearer and dearer to my heart than anyone on this planet, invites that very same ranger over to eat soup in our kitchen."

"Oh, that's why you're mad," she muttered. "Thought it might be something else."

Before she could escape back to her couch, I spun around. "If you think I'm jealous then I'm sorry to disappoint you, Nana. I have Cade, and frankly, the more I get to know him, the more I realize he's the only man for me. In fact, I'm heading over to his house just as soon as I'm done here."

Nana's smile was slightly condescending. "Well, then that's perfect, Button."

"I'm serious. You can match those two up and even have a wedding right here in the cottage. I'll bake them a cake. There—proof enough that I couldn't care less about your matchmaking scheme?"

"Proof enough for me." There was still far too much amusement in her tone.

I finished the dishes, put the leftover soup in the refrigerator and hurried in to take a shower.

The porch light glowed over Cade's front door. I knocked once and walked right inside. Music floated out from the kitchen area. Cade's portable speaker and phone were sitting on the counter. He was washing dishes.

"Hey, Ramone, I'm almost done. I let these pile up all day, and I realized I was out of glasses and forks, so I had no choice except to wash them. Glass of wine?" he asked.

"Actually, a cold beer sounds better." I walked over to the refrigerator.

"Pop one open for the dishwasher too, eh?"

I opened up two beers and walked over to the sink. I picked up a dishtowel to start drying.

"So, tell me about your day." It didn't seem like a "how's it going" question. There was something more prying in it.

"Uh, well, there was the dead body that I texted you about." I wasn't sure where he was going with his line of questioning, so I kept details scarce.

"Yes, those types of texts always warm my heart. Somehow

or another, my girlfriend always winds up in the close vicinity of a dead body."

There was just enough wryness in his tone to make me set down the towel and glass I was holding. "All right, what gives?"

Cade placed the last bowl on the dishrack and snatched the towel from me to dry his hands. He stared at me as he finished the task.

"You heard that I was a suspect," I said.

"I didn't hear. I was an actual alibi corroborator."

The air rushed out of me like a deflating balloon. "Dalton came here?"

"Apparently, he had a checklist of people you visited this morning." He dropped the towel on the counter, picked up both beers, handed me mine and motioned for me to follow him to the table. "What on earth is going on? Braddock was his usual disagreeable, charmless self. He wouldn't give any details. It was all very official," Cade said the last part in a stern, sharp tone. "He asked if I saw you between the hours of nine and twelve this morning."

"What did you tell him?"

"Hmm, that I had no idea what he was talking about because I hadn't seen you all morning." His teasing smile was annoyingly appealing.

"Well then, if my alibi has broken down, I might as well just turn myself in."

We both paused to drink some beer. It tasted good after the spicy lentil soup. "Seriously, why was he checking your alibi?"

"Isn't it perfectly clear? I'm a suspect in his murder investigation. I found the body, and one of my bakery napkins was found underneath Roberta."

"Well then, he should get alibis for the majority of people in town. We've all got those napkins jammed in our pockets and fluttering around in our cars."

I smiled. "I know. Isn't it awesome?"

"What motive could you possibly have had to kill the woman? Hold that thought—I need salt with this beer." Cade got up, grabbed a bag of pretzels out of the pantry and returned to the table. "Now, where were we? That's right—motive."

"Well, it's a flimsy motive to say the least. I know several other people who had much more reason to kill Roberta Schubert than me. Roberta was planning on opening a teahouse in town, and she was going to serve traditional English scones and clotted cream. She made a point of letting me know that it would probably put a dent in my business, and frankly, she might have been right. She was selling scones at her yard sale all weekend, and my business was way down."

"Ah, the competition motive," Cade said. "I see. Then it seems he has plenty of reason to lock you up. Guess it's good I covered for you." He winked.

"Easy for you to make light of it. You weren't the one marched down to the station to sit in that drab, cold interrogation room."

Some of the amusement in his expression faded. "He put you in the interrogation room? What a clown. Was it just the two of you in the room?"

I tilted my head at him. "No, there were two other detectives and my lawyer. Yes, just the two of us. What are you implying?"

Cade sat back, defeated. "You're right. Sorry. I guess I'm just angry that he put you in that damn room in the first place."

"As he told me numerous times—he was just doing his job. And I'm extra mad at him because I told him to check with

Roxi's niece, Tanya, and Regina about my alibi. I saw them before I came here. I didn't want him to bring you into it."

"Why not?" Cade looked hurt.

"I just didn't want—I prefer it when—" I groaned in frustration. The correct words were failing me, but Cade stared at me unblinking waiting for me to explain.

"I'd just rather you two didn't meet up—ever. There's far too much friction between you. I was sure he'd skip asking you anything."

"Guess he wanted to come and act official, chest out and chin jutting." Cade straightened, puffed out his chest like an angry rooster and squared his jaw to demonstrate.

"Yes, because you've certainly never acted like an angry rooster around him." I picked up the beer and was seriously considering a second one. It had been quite a day, and even this part, the part I'd been looking most forward to, felt stiff and scratchy.

"I have no need to act like a rooster. I'm clearly the superior being ... in every way. And I got the girl ... as they say in the movies." He reached for my hand, but I wasn't inclined to give it. He lowered his hand dejectedly. "Or at least I used to have her."

I relented and gave him my hand. It was impossible to stay angry at the man. Those hazel eyes and the crooked, cocky grin got me every time. "Let's drop this subject. I was hoping this would be the least trying part of my day."

Cade stood and helped me to my feet. He wrapped his arms around me. "I say we restart this whole thing. Good evening, my love, how was your—" He stopped. "Nope, not going to make that mistake again. I've got a much better idea." He pulled me closer for a kiss.

twenty-four
. . .

THE BAKERY WAS CLOSED on Mondays, so I used that day for paperwork. It was the one day when I wasn't elbow-deep in dough and batter and stickiness. I didn't mind being at work on my day off. It was kind of nice to sit in my office and stare out at the kitchen with its gleaming worktables and ovens. This whole dream had turned out even better than I'd imagined. A wicked thought crossed my mind, and while I was disappointed and angry at myself for thinking it, I couldn't avoid it. Roberta would no longer be selling scones and clotted cream, so business would most likely return to normal.

I quickly fanned the air around me to push away any bad karma my thought might have produced, then I set to work filling out the week's purchase orders. I wasn't far into the task when I heard the front door open. At first it alarmed me because I knew I'd locked it, but Jack had a unique way of walking on his big, heavy boots. One leg always struck the floor heavier than the other. He told me his uneven gait was the result of a bad knee injury while playing football in high school.

I popped out of the office. "Jack, what brings you here on your day off?"

"Isn't it your day off, too?"

"Just paperwork. Did you get my message?" I asked. I'd found time during my hectic Sunday to send Jack a text. I'd told him to call me when he got a chance.

"I didn't get it, and the reason I didn't is because I left my phone—" He paused and opened the cupboard he used for his personal belongings, then retrieved his phone. "I looked all over my house and car, and I thought well, Jack, it's time to face it—you're losing your mind. Then I remembered that I'd put it in here while I cleaned up, and I walked out without it. In my defense—I did spend most of my life without one of these things glued to my body. It was actually kind of nice not having it all day yesterday, other than the fretful time I spent looking for it and thinking I was really starting to lose my mind." He glanced at the phone. "And there it is. A text from the boss. What's up? Did I miss anything while I was out fishing?"

"Well, let's see," I said airily. "We didn't sell out of cinnamon rolls or pecan buns."

"Didn't—as in did not? That's a first. Did it have to do with Roberta's scones?"

"Yes, she was still selling them at her yard sale. So, I thought, well, I'll take a few extra over to her to show her no hard feelings and let her know I welcomed the competition."

Jack grabbed a bottle of water from the office mini fridge. "That was good of you."

"Only I didn't get a chance to tell her because Roberta was dead when I got there."

He froze halfway before getting the bottle to his mouth. "Dead? Seriously? Was it a heart attack? She seemed like someone who could work herself right into a heart attack."

"She was strangled."

Jack lowered the bottle and looked properly shocked. "This town is so picture-perfect most of the time, but it sure has a dark underbelly. Do they know who did it?"

"Well, after my alibi was checked out—"

Jack choked on the water. He pressed the back of his hand to his mouth to stifle the cough and catch his breath. "You were a suspect?" he asked with wide eyes.

"I was. I found the body, and one of our napkins was underneath Roberta."

"And Braddock thought that was enough to consider you a suspect?"

"I guess so. He mentioned I had motive because he knew my business had slowed because of her impromptu scone sale and that I was worried her teahouse would affect the bakery."

"I'm finding it hard to believe that Ranger Braddock, even for the slightest moment, considered you a murder suspect."

"I'm having a hard time wrapping my mind around it, too." I straightened out the papers on my desk. "Well, just about finished here. What are your plans for the rest of the day?"

"Need to tackle some yardwork, then I'm going to make myself a tray of lasagna."

"Yummy. Enjoy and I'll see you in the morning."

"Yep, bright and early," he called on his way out.

I finished my work and grabbed my purse. I hadn't decided which direction to go next on the investigation. The decision was made for me. I was just locking up when I spotted Mallory heading into the market. I had a few more questions for her.

I crossed the street. The smells of peppery sliced meats and red onions hit me as I walked inside. Tanya was behind the sandwich counter, fixing sandwiches for several customers. Mallory was in the produce section running her nose past a cantaloupe.

Roxi was stocking the potato chip rack. She glanced around to see who'd walked in. "Scottie, I guess I missed a few events while I was at home painting my back bedroom."

I stopped in front of her. "Let me guess—you painted it a plum color?"

She looked up, surprised. "How did you know?"

I pointed out the streak of plum on the heel of her thumb.

"Darn, I thought I got all of it." She started rubbing the splotch of paint.

"I'll bet it looks great."

"Meh, I liked the color better on the color sample. Now it feels a bit too—purple." She was still rubbing her thumb as she pushed up from her crouched position. "I was shocked to hear about Roberta Schubert and even more shocked to hear that Dalton was here checking on your alibi." She gave up on the purple thumb. "He wasn't seriously considering you as a suspect?"

I shrugged. "If I didn't know him—if I was just a stranger—it would've been easy to see why he started with me as the first person of interest. Without going into details of the case, there were some circumstances and evidence that could have led him to that conclusion. Fortunately, I was out and about delivering cinnamon rolls."

"Yes, I heard you brought some in. My one day off, of course."

I laughed. "I'll bring you some next Sunday. I need to talk to Mallory. I can't wait to see the purple room."

"It might not be purple for long," she said as she pulled bags of barbecue chips out of a box.

Mallory had moved on to the bananas. She spotted me as she placed a bunch in her basket. "Scottie, have you heard any more about Roberta's death? I'm still trying to absorb it."

I reached her, and she frowned. "I'm feeling ashamed because more than once since I heard the news, I've thought maybe it shouldn't be so surprising. Roberta always managed to ruffle feathers. We were friends for a long time, but she definitely fell into that new category—now what's it called? The category of friend that they say you should dump immediately for your mental wellbeing."

"Toxic friends?" I asked.

Mallory snapped her fingers. "That's it. Roberta never built you up, you know, like a good friend would be apt to do. She only liked to degrade and insult. She really was mean."

"I had a feeling that she was not the easiest person to get along with. I suppose the two of you made a friendship work because you are much easier going."

Mallory smiled at the compliment. "I used to tell her 'don't take yourself so seriously, Roberta' and boy, did that make her mad."

"You know, now that I'm here with you—I wanted to ask you something else."

Her face blanched. "I know. Ranger Braddock has asked me to come in this afternoon to answer some questions. I sure hope he's just asking for the chat so I can tell him more about Roberta. I was very angry at her, but I certainly would never have thought of killing her."

My mind darted to something more aggravating. Dalton set an appointment for Mallory to come in on her own for questioning. I bet she wasn't even going to be taken into that horrid interrogation room. Mallory had much more reason to kill Roberta than me.

"Do you think he's going to arrest me?" she asked, breaking through my thoughts.

"No, I'm sure he just wants information, but be sure to tell him you showed up to talk to her yesterday morning, and that she wasn't at the yard sale. If you keep any information back that will look suspicious."

"You're so right. I'll let him know first thing."

"About your visit to the Schubert house yesterday morning—did you see anyone else? Did you notice anyone parked in front of the yard or walking on the sidewalk or maybe standing in a neighbor's yard?"

Mallory was shaking her head and then she held up a finger as if a lightbulb went off. "When I was walking to my car, I saw Arnie Morris walking up the sidewalk. He was sort of walking like this." She bent her arms and moved her elbows back and forth. "You know—like someone on a mission or with a purpose. I waved at him, but he was too lost in his thoughts to notice me. I assumed he was going to the Schubert's house, but I didn't stick around to find out. I got in my car and drove away."

"I see. Well, I'll let you get back to your fruit selection. By the way, the strawberries are delicious right now."

"Great, maybe I'll buy some. Thanks."

I waved goodbye to Roxi as I left. My trip across to the market had paid off. Arnie had lied to me. He never mentioned going back to Roberta's house. I wondered what else he was lying about.

twenty-five
. . .

"HERE YOU GO, Nana, ham and cheese with mustard." I placed the sandwich in front of her. "Do you want some juice or iced tea to go with it?"

"Button, you know I love you more than anything in this world, but you're treating me like a five-year-old. I certainly could have made my own sandwich with one hand. This is your day off. I'm sure you have better things to do than sit around and coddle your old grandmother."

"First of all, making a sandwich with one hand would not be an easy task. Secondly, as I've said before, it's nice being able to take care of you for a change. Thirdly, your arm will be mended soon enough and then you can go back to making my sandwiches. And fourth—" I tapped my chin and rolled up my eyes in thought. "Where was I going with this? Oh, that's right—I do have some place to be. I'm working on Roberta's murder case, but please don't tell your bestie, Dalton."

The lines on her forehead deepened. "What's a bestie? Never

It was my day off, and I should have been going on a hike or a bike ride to take advantage of the incredible weather. Instead, I'd tasked myself with finding Roberta's killer. I could ask myself why I bothered, but I knew the answer. I felt slighted by Dalton, and I wanted to show him up. I wanted to show him that I could do his job better. Oh jeez, was Nana right? Was I overreacting because Dalton had hurt my feelings?

"Argh, Nana and her grandmother-honed psychological warfare," I muttered as I turned the corner onto Arnie's street. She always looked so sweet and innocent sitting wrapped in her knitted shawls and with her cookie jar full of oatmeal gems. But there were far more layers to her than the grandmotherly exterior. I had many layers, too, and she knew how to get beneath and between each and every one of them.

A trailer loaded with boxes was hitched to Arnie's car. The front door opened as I walked up to it. Arnie stepped out, grunting as he held a large, heavy box.

I rushed forward to help him. "Here let me take this side," I said.

His head popped up over the box. "Oh, thanks, Scottie. It was heavier than I expected."

I had the unenviable position of walking backward over a yard I didn't know well. I nearly twisted an ankle as the pathway ended and the lawn began, but after a few near drops, we managed to get the box onto the trailer.

Arnie's face was red from carrying the heavy box. He patted the top of it. "My books."

"That explains it."

Arnie pulled a cloth out of his back pocket and wiped his brow. "What brings you back here? Twice in as many days," he added with a suspicious squint.

"I'll just be frank, Arnie. I'm trying to find out who killed Roberta. I was the one who found her, so I have a stake in the whole thing."

Arnie nodded but the suspicion hadn't left his face. "I guess, like me, you're one of the people who will benefit from Roberta's death."

My posture tightened.

"I've been writing a murder mystery between freelance assignments, so you'll have to excuse me. I've got murder on my mind. I heard she was strangled. Harry told me when I called to offer my condolences. Her planned teahouse would've been competition for your bakery."

"Wow, you really do have murder on your mind. You're right. Ranger Braddock has already spoken to me and ruled me out because I have an alibi. On the other hand, you never mentioned to me that you went to Roberta's house yesterday morning. In fact, you told me you were here packing boxes."

"Hmm, good sleuthing. I'm impressed."

"Thanks."

"You've heard right. I did go there yesterday morning hoping to talk Roberta out of the eviction. I'd started packing up my things, and it all felt so overwhelming, moving my life into storage and looking for a new place."

"Did you talk to her?"

"Nope, she wasn't around. I guess the killer had already gotten to her. I waited a few minutes and considered going up to the door, but I didn't want to get stuck in a conversation with Harry like I had on Saturday. I knew I'd get nowhere with him. Roberta led that man around by the nose. Have you spoken to him? He's the one with the real motive. Years of being belittled and bossed around—it'd be enough to make any man crack."

I hadn't expected the turn in conversation, and I wanted to kick myself for not considering that as a motive in the first place. I wasn't getting any killer vibes from Arnie, but he'd given me a new person of interest.

"So, you left Roberta's house and—"

"Came back here and as you can see,"—he waved at the loaded trailer—"I got serious about packing up. That was before I knew Roberta was dead. If I had killed her, then why would I go through all the trouble? Harry surely would have let me stay since Roberta's plans would have died with her."

"But you didn't mention it when I spoke to you."

Arnie shrugged. "I got the feeling you might be fishing for information, so I figured that Roberta's death had been anything but natural."

"And you didn't want me to know that you'd been there because it would have been incriminating."

"Exactly." He tilted his head in question. "Why were you there on Sunday?"

"Good question. I was bringing Roberta some cinnamon rolls to let her know I had no hard feelings about her future teahouse. That was when Harry came out of the house, upset and worried because he couldn't find her. Do you really think he could have done it?"

"Maybe Harry's a really good actor," he suggested.

"That's entirely possible. Well, I won't keep you. You're obviously extremely busy."

"Thanks for your help with the book box. Your timing was perfect." Arnie scrunched his brows and looked past me. "Wonder what he wants? I suppose I could make an educated guess."

I looked over my shoulder. It was Dalton. I turned back to

Arnie. "Just be honest. See you later." I walked down the driveway and met Dalton as he walked up.

He lifted his sunglasses and gazed down at me. "Scottie, what are you doing here?"

I pointed my thumb over my shoulder. "I was helping Arnie move some heavy boxes."

Dalton wasn't buying it. "Scottie, you need to stay out of this investigation."

"Yes, sir. I'll leave you to *your job*." I could feel his stern glower on my back as I hurried past him to my car.

twenty-six
. . .

I PARKED in front of Regina's shop and glanced across the street at the bakery. A few people, strangers, not locals, were trying to peer in the windows. "It'll be open tomorrow," I called to them.

They looked disappointed as they waved weakly and continued toward the bookstore. I stepped inside Regina's shop. She had a very perfumy stick of lavender incense burning in a ceramic pot on her checkout counter. I could hear her in the back, rummaging through something, a newspaper possibly. "Be right with you," she called.

"Only me, Regina," I called back.

Regina pushed a stray strand of hair out of her eyes. She had the rest of her hair tied up in a scarf. "I'm trying to organize my holiday gift wrap, so I can put it in storage."

"I thought I heard you moving paper around."

Regina crinkled her nose, then sneezed. "That is far too strong. I was trying a new brand of incense, but incense should be subtle. This stuff smells like the industrial cleaners they use in public restrooms." She blew on the incense, which only made the stick glow brighter and put off more noxious scent. Now it was my turn to sneeze.

Regina picked up the stick and smashed the lit end into the ceramic holder to extinguish it. The leftover smell was almost worse than the burning one. She rolled her eyes. "That company is never going to make it. They had a nice brochure, and the saleswoman was very charming, an earthy type with long wavy hair and sandals, but no way. That is terrible incense, and that was lavender, the scent that's usually the mildest." She pushed aside the smoking incense holder. "What brings you here today?" She looked pointedly at my empty hands.

"Sorry, no cinnamon rolls today. Nana mentioned that you grew up with the Fairburn sisters, Roberta and Janice."

"I did. I was mostly friendly with Janice. Roberta was a grade below and not nearly as likable."

"Yes, I've heard that. I also noticed that the two sisters weren't very chummy. Do you know what happened between them?"

Regina laughed happily. We were on her favorite topic—gossip. "Well, it was such a long time ago now, but I think some of it was the obvious—they were very different. And, of course, there is no law that says you have to get along with a sibling. I remember going to parties and things with Janice, but she never invited her younger sister to tag along. And, as you know, after high school, I went across the country for college, and I was in Boston for a few years after that." She rubbed her temple and once again pushed away the loose strand of hair. "When I got back to Ripple Creek, I was surprised to find out that Harry and Roberta had gotten married."

"Oh? Why is that?"

Regina shuffled forward with an excited gleam in her eye. "Well, in high school, Harry and Janice were a couple. They were quite smitten. Back then, getting married right out of high school was very popular, and the two of them had been planning to do just that. Then, off I went on my short adventure. When I returned, Harry and Roberta were married. Janice had left town. She returned a few years later." Regina smiled at me fondly. "I guess we all come tiptoeing back eventually, once we realize that the outside world doesn't have nearly as much to offer as our beloved town."

"I guess so. Did you ever find out what happened between all of them? Did you get a sense it was a love triangle back in high school?"

"Gosh, I sure never picked up on that. Like I said, Harry and Janice were so in love. I never noticed anything between Roberta and Harry. I brought it up to Janice once, but she cut me right off, saying she didn't want to talk about it. Why so many questions about the sisters?" Regina's eyes rounded. "Dalton was in here asking about your visit on Sunday morning. I thought it was strange, but he didn't want to provide details. Roberta was murdered, wasn't she?"

"I'm afraid so."

Regina then seemed to put the two things together. A dry laugh shot from her mouth. "You're not telling me that Dalton was here checking on—"

"My alibi. Yes, he was, but Regina, I'd appreciate it if you didn't tell anyone. It's all rather embarrassing." I knew I was probably blowing into the wind because Regina would be dying to tell someone. I was counting on the fact that she adored my grandmother and considered Nana her best friend. "Nana would appreciate it, too," I added for extra security.

Regina pulled an invisible zipper across her lips, which didn't mean much. I'd seen her make the same gesture more than once, only to immediately blow right through that invisible zipper to spread gossip. And she proved my point instantly, only this gossip had nothing to do with me—technically.

"I hear that Tanya was quite taken with Dalton. Evie had them for dinner, and they enjoyed each other's company."

"Did you hear that from my matchmaking grandmother?" I asked.

"No, from Tanya. I think she's interested. We'll have to see if it goes both ways. I think they'll make a fine couple. What do you think?" I couldn't believe how incredibly awkward it felt having to discuss Dalton's potential love life.

"I have no idea. I guess time will tell." I was more interested in the weird love triangle between Harry, Roberta and Janice. Did Janice and Harry part ways after high school? Still, it seemed strange that Roberta would swoop right in and take her sister's place. Then again, there probably wasn't a large catalogue of young singles in Ripple Creek back then.

"Thanks for the information, Regina."

"Anytime." And I knew that to be very true. "Oh, and do let me know if you need another alibi. Always happy to help." She winked.

I waved. "You'll be the first to know." I stepped out into the wonderful sunshine and once again lamented that I was spending my day on a murder investigation instead of a hike. I had another stop to make. It was time to visit Harry Schubert. There seemed to be far more to him than tears and hand-wringing.

twenty-seven
. . .

I REACHED HARRY'S HOUSE. The yard sale items were still strewn across the yard. Everything looked very picked over as if people had just been helping themselves. I had a nice excuse for the visit. I would offer to help clean up the mess on the front lawn. I'd always found kindness worked well when you were trying to get a suspect to open up. Dalton always had a disadvantage there because his uniform assured people he wasn't there for a friendly visit. Arnie knew as soon as he spotted Dalton that he was going to be questioned about the murder.

A text came through before I could get out of the car. It was Cade. He was busy working, so I hadn't spoken to him all day. "My laptop and I were about to have a big raging fight, so I snapped it shut and walked away to cool off. What are you up to today?"

"Nothing much. Just trying to clear my good name of murder."

The phone rang. After spending all day on his keyboard, Cade never liked to have long text conversations. I answered.

"Are you still a suspect?" he asked with worry.

"No, I'm being dramatic. I don't think I'm a suspect, but who knows. I'm out talking to the few people, other than the town's madwoman baker, who might have had motive to kill Roberta. Since you're angry at the laptop, I assume you aren't having a good day writing."

"Let's just say I've written a lot of gibberish and not good gibberish either."

"Is gibberish ever considered good?" I asked.

"See, now you have me questioning my entire mastery of the English language."

"Sounds like you need a nice dinner. Come by the house around six, and I'll come up with something brilliant to take the edge off."

"I'll be there, and now, I think I'll head outside to weed the garden. It's a mindless activity, and clearing my head might help with the book."

"Wear gloves. The snakes are out of hibernation." I glanced up toward the house. Harry shuffled out to his front stoop, looked forlornly at the yard sale mess and went back inside. He was certainly still wearing a mask of profound grief.

"Now pulling weeds is no longer a mindless task because my mind will be filled with snakes."

I giggled. "Oops, sorry but it's true. They're always extra active in spring. Just put on gloves."

"Right, my gardening gloves only go to my wrists. What about the rest of me?"

"That's why I told you to look out for snakes. Love ya."

"Why did that sound like a sendoff?"

"Cuz it was. I've got a suspect in my sights, and I need to investigate."

"Fine, I'll go outside and have a chat with the venomous reptiles slinking around the yard just waiting for my winter-white tender flesh to tempt them. Love ya, too."

"See you later."

I got out of the car and headed up to the door. Harry answered after a few knocks. He looked terrible, pale and frail. He was wearing the same clothes I'd seen him in the day before, and gray beard stubble dotted his chin.

"Scottie, I'm sorry, I'm not really prepared for visitors."

"No, of course not. I stopped by to see if I could be of some assistance. I thought I might start clearing the yard sale away."

"Well, that's very kind of you. I can't ask you to do that. I was going to eat some lunch and then do it myself. The table with her scones and cream—" His voice trailed off, and he pushed his hand against his mouth to stop himself from crying. "It's covered with ants. And the memorial is tomorrow."

"A memorial?" I asked.

"Yes, Janice is letting people know. We're going to say a few words about my dear Roberta and sing her favorite songs." He perked up. "Actually, maybe you could help us out."

"Absolutely. Anything you need."

"Come into the house, please. It's rude of me to keep you standing on the stoop. I apologize. I'm not myself."

I followed him inside. His shoulders were slumped, and he had the posture of a man who'd just suffered a grave loss. Nothing about him said killer. His grief seemed genuine. Either that or he was one heck of an actor.

He led me to the kitchen. There were a few dirty dishes on the counter, cereal bowls mostly.

"I could fix you some lunch," I said.

"That's kind of you but no. I've got something in the freezer I can heat." Harry walked over to a pink recipe box and flipped open the lid. "Here it is, right up front." He pulled out a card, and a weak smile crossed his face. "I can only imagine what my Roberta would say if she knew I was handing this to *you* of all people."

I took the handwritten card from his hand. "Mother's Scones" was written across the top. Roberta's writing was pretty with lots of curls and flourishes. I looked at Harry in question. "I don't understand."

"I know it's strange for me to be handing you this recipe, but I thought it would be nice to have some of her scones at the memorial. Do you think you could make a few dozen? I know it's a lot to ask, and of course, I'll pay you back for the ingredients."

"Nonsense. I'd be happy to make the scones. The clotted cream—well—I've never made it, but I know it takes some time to make."

"Yes, don't worry about the cream." He walked over to a cupboard and pulled open the door. There were at least a dozen jars of bright red strawberry jam on the shelves. Each jar had a label with Roberta's writing and a strawberry sticker. "We'll just serve them with her homemade jam. Now, you're sure about this? I know it's short notice."

"I'm happy to do it. How is Janice doing?" I asked.

"As well as could be expected, I suppose. She's organizing the memorial, which I'm thankful for."

"I've heard that you and Janice were high school sweethearts. Is that true?" It wasn't my smoothest transition, but I wanted to get to the heart of the matter.

Harry shrugged as he closed the jam cupboard. "That was such a long time ago." He turned around, and there was a slight sparkle in his eyes as if he'd drifted back to his high school days. "We were always together. I was sure we'd get married, then Janice broke it off without ever really explaining why. She left town suddenly, and Roberta was here to pick up the pieces. She was very good to me. She knew my heart was broken. Roberta and I fell in love eventually and got married soon after."

"I'm so glad Roberta was there to help you through all of that. Excuse me for saying, but it seemed the two sisters weren't all that close."

He chuckled. "You could say that again. They never had anything in common. Janice and I managed to repair our relationship enough to be friends. We were in-laws, after all, so it was for the best. I can tell you I was nuts about her in high school. She'd walk into a classroom, and all the heads would turn, and boy, was I proud to have her on my arm." His face lit up as he spoke about those days.

"What about Roberta?"

"You mean in high school? She was a quiet sort, not terribly popular. Not like Janice." Harry paused, dropped his head and took a tissue out of his sleeve. "Can't seem to stop the tears."

I walked over and patted him on the shoulder. "It'll get easier with time. In the meantime, I'm going to go outside and start clearing away the mess. Should I put everything in the garage?"

"Yes, that's very thoughtful of you, Scottie. Thank you. I know Roberta wasn't very kind to you. She was determined to get that business up and running, and I think she worried you were her biggest hurdle in making it a success."

"That's crazy. People were lining up for her scones."

"Well, I suppose it doesn't matter now. There'll be no teahouse."

I walked to the door. Harry followed me to unlock the garage. "I saw Arnie earlier. He's moving out of your rental."

"Yes, I tried to talk him into staying. Roberta always handled the rental. I don't know the first thing about it." We reached the garage. I spotted Oscar, Harry's neighbor, out watering his flower beds. He glanced our direction and waved weakly. There was yellow caution tape hung across his garden gate.

"Harry, how was Roberta's relationship with Oscar and Paula?"

Harry stopped and nodded at his neighbor. "It was all right. We didn't speak much. They keep mostly to themselves. Roberta complained to them once that their sprinklers were hitting our car, and that sort of ended any prospect of an amiable relationship." Harry opened the garage. "Just put everything in the middle, and I'll sort it out once I can think straight. Can I interest you in a frozen bowl of ravioli?"

"No thanks. I'll get started on the yard."

"I'll be out to help you in a few minutes. Just need some food." He started to walk away, then stopped and turned back. "Thank you, Scottie. I'm feeling slightly more human after this visit. I think cleaning up the yard will help."

"Glad to hear it, Harry."

Harry walked back to the house, and I stared out at the rather large task I'd just given myself. And I was no closer to solving the murder. Harry seemed to genuinely love his wife, so there was no motive.

I walked over to the first table and used an old milk crate to start collecting the trinkets on the table. The recipe card was sticking out of my pocket reminding me that I'd given myself more than one task on my day off.

twenty-eight
. . .

THERE WASN'T anything too unique about Roberta's scone recipe. It contained the usual ingredients—flour, baking powder, salt, sugar, butter and milk. The technique was standard, too—mixing the dry ingredients, cutting in the butter and then mixing it with milk to form a dough. Even with baking a homemade pizza in-between, I managed to get the scones mixed, shaped and ready to bake in less than an hour.

Nana came in from a short walk in the neighborhood with Hannah. Her cheeks were pink from the exercise and brisk early evening air. She looked much better now that she'd added walks back into her routine.

"Sit and I'll pour you some iced tea," I said.

Nana was slightly out of breath, so she gladly took a seat at the table. "We decided to pick up the pace this round because the sun was setting. How are the scones coming?" she asked.

"Ready to go into the oven once I brush them with the egg wash." I whisked an egg into a frothy liquid, poured in a splash of milk and brushed the scones before sliding them into the oven.

"I can't wait for the pizza," Nana said between sips of cold tea. "That oregano has my mouth watering. It's nice of you to make those scones for the memorial. You mentioned you spoke to Harry about his past with the sisters. I knew the girls mostly from when they helped their mom out at the teahouse, and I never really knew about their social lives. Regina, on the other hand, went to school with them. I'll bet she was thrilled to relay some gossip about the sisters."

"She practically jumped out of her shoes at the chance." I used a chiffonade slicing technique to create thin ribbons of basil. An earthy, almost licorice-y scent filled the air. Basil was Cade's favorite herb.

A knock on the door sent my grandmother rocketing out of her seat. "That'll be Cade." She wore a big smile as she left the kitchen. I heard her in the front room talking animatedly, almost flirtatiously, and in between I heard the deep, soothing sound of Cade's voice. I'd grown very fond of it, of the whole man, top to bottom, for that matter.

Nana came in with a bouquet of orange roses. "Look what Cade brought me. Wasn't that sweet?"

I smiled at Cade. "That was very sweet."

"And the sweetness does not stop there," he announced as he held up a box of chocolates.

I placed my hand demurely against my chest. "For lil ole me? And it's not even my birthday." I dropped the southern twang and walked over to kiss him lightly. "Thank you for the chocolates. We can have them after pizza. Sit. I'll get you a glass of iced tea." I poured him a glass and set it in front of him.

"Well, you'll be happy to hear that I didn't encounter any

snakes while pulling weeds." He held up his hand. "But you should have warned me about bees being angered by the intrusion in their garden." There was a quarter-sized red bump on the side of his hand.

"I assumed bees were a given. Did you take some antihistamine?" I asked.

"No, I'm sure my great-grandfather, Arthur, would have frowned upon me taking the easy way out. I scraped out the stinger and carried on—like a true pioneer."

Nana laughed. "Somehow, you don't really fit my vision of a true pioneer. An elegant landowner maybe, but pioneer, no."

Cade sighed dejectedly. "There went the vision I conjured in my head of me in dirt-stained overalls pounding nails into my broken wagon wheel all while fighting off angry bees. Something smells delicious."

"I'm baking scones for tomorrow's memorial," I said.

"Right. I was at the market earlier, and a woman there was handing Roxi some flyers. I was sure it was for a yard sale or block party or something happy, so I was a little surprised when I saw it was for a memorial." Cade pulled a folded paper out of his pocket. "She handed me one before she walked out. She said the memorial was for her sister. Your murder victim, I presume."

"I'd prefer it if you didn't call her *my* murder victim, but yes, that must have been Janice." I took hold of the flyer. It had been printed on paper with a sunflower border. Even the font she'd used seemed more suited to a summer garden party than a memorial. "Come celebrate the life of our beloved Roberta. Six o'clock at the Schubert residence. Refreshments will be provided."

Cade watched me as I read the flyer out loud. I stopped and must have made a face because he pointed at me. "See, that was my reaction. Quite jovial for a memorial service. The sunflowers were an interesting touch. Didn't the woman just die yesterday? Her sister was in quite good spirits considering."

I put down the flyer. "The two sisters weren't close."

There was another knock at the door. I knew it was Hannah before opening it. She'd seen Cade's car and decided to show up unexpectedly. I also knew before she walked inside that she'd pretend to be surprised and apologetic and explain that she had no idea we had company. I didn't mind. She was smitten with Cade, and frankly, I couldn't blame her.

I opened the door. "Evening, Scottie. I thought I'd drop by to make sure that Evie got home all right." Our house was literally half a block from Hannah's.

"She sure did. She's in the kitchen. We're having pizza if you'd like to stay." She made a beeline for the kitchen before I could finish the invite. And then came the big, fake apology.

"I'm so sorry. I didn't know you had company."

"Nonsense," I said (like always). "Pull up a seat. We're drinking iced tea."

Again, Hannah was already settled in the seat next to Cade before I could finish. "Oh, those roses," Hannah sighed. Nana had placed them in a glass vase in the center of the table.

"Aren't they beautiful?" Nana asked. "Cade brought them for me." It was adorable to watch both of them gush over Cade. I winked secretly at him and handed Hannah a tea.

Hannah spotted the flyer on the table. "Did you see this?" she asked us, which seemed unnecessary given that the flyer was sitting right in the middle of the table. "Poor Roberta. Poor Janice. Poor Harry."

I had a full kitchen and another opportunity to ask questions of someone who had a long history in town and who was just a step below Regina when it came to retaining and relaying gossip.

"Hannah, do you remember the sisters when they were younger?" I asked. I joined the rest at the table while I waited for the scones to bake.

"Of course I do." Hannah was a decade younger than Nana, but she looked the same age. "Janice was such a pretty thing, with long braids and flawless skin. She used to help her mom at the teahouse, and she was always pleasant and polite. Roberta was much shyer, less friendly but also polite."

"Do you remember anything about the relationship between Janice and Harry? They were a couple in high school."

"Gosh, I do remember talking to their mother about it once. She said Janice was heartbroken when Harry broke it off."

I sat up straighter and utterly confused. "Wait. Harry broke it off?"

"Yes, I believe so. Eleanor was upset that Roberta showed him so much kindness after he broke her sister's heart. She was even more shocked that they ended up getting married, but by then, the breakup was far enough in the past that it didn't matter as much. Janice had left town to pursue a career, and Roberta married Harry."

"You're sure that Harry ended it?"

I'd asked it enough to cause Hannah to question herself. She pressed her fingers to her mouth. "I think that's right. Maybe I've had the whole thing wrong all this time." She rolled her eyes up in thought. "No, I think that it was Harry who ended it."

"Had you heard differently?" Cade asked. "Maybe that person got it wrong."

"It's possible, only my other source was Harry himself. He

told me Janice left him, and he was very broken up about it. Roberta swept in to pick up the pieces."

"Well, that seems like something he'd remember," Nana said.

I nodded. "It does indeed."

The oven timer rang. "The scones are ready. Now I can bake the pizza. Extra cheese all right with everyone?"

"Never say no to extra cheese," Nana said.

"Here, here." Cade lifted his glass, and Hannah and Nana both raced to be the first to tap his glass with theirs.

twenty-nine

. . .

THE EARLY MORNING had started with a cold rain. Both Jack and I showed up dressed head to toe in rain gear, and I had to mop the floor after we'd shed our dripping outer layers. Aside from that rough start, the day got rolling, and the sun eventually poked through. Business had improved again, and after the first hour, we were nearly out of Danish, and our bread stock was down by half.

The shop was clear for the first time, so Jack and I stopped for a coffee break. It was our first break of the day and well-deserved. "I saw a rather sunshiny flyer, cheery and bright, but it was for Roberta's memorial," Jack said.

"Yes, her sister, Janice handed those out. Roberta's husband, Harry, asked me to bake scones for the event, using her mother's traditional scone recipe."

"There is nothing more confusing than baked good terminology between the US and the UK. I know they've got the market cornered on scones, and our scones have been Americanized to an almost comical level." Jack poured cream into his coffee. "The other day I saw a recipe for a salted caramel scone. Looked delicious, only it seemed about as far removed from being a scone as a brownie. Scones have a big history in the British Isles, but to me they're a slightly sweet biscuit. Only their version of 'a biscuit' is our version of a cookie. I wonder if they refer to anything as a cookie?"

"That sounds like a purely American term." The front door opened. "I'll get it. You stay on break. It's been a long morning."

I was surprised to find Janice standing in the shop. I knew she was busy with the memorial. "Janice, good morning. How are you doing?"

"Fine, thanks," she said cheerily as if her sister hadn't just been murdered. She seemed to remember right then, as if she'd read my thoughts, that she was in mourning. Her face drooped, and her shoulders followed. "This is much harder than I expected. Roberta and I didn't talk or hang out much, but she was still my sister and my only remaining family. And poor Harry is beside himself."

"If you see him, let him know that I made three dozen scones for the memorial."

Janice shrugged shyly and added in a smile. "I hope we get that many people. Roberta wasn't exactly popular in town. I talked to Harry several times, telling him he should talk her out of the teahouse. People loved my mother. That's why her shop did so well. Oh well, I guess that's not important anymore. My dear sister will never be able to fulfill that dream." She paused to collect herself, then took a bracing breath. "I came here to talk about the scones. I dropped by Harry's house this morning. He mentioned that you were a big help clearing the yard for today's memorial. Thank you so much for that."

"I was glad to help. How was Harry this morning? He seemed to feel better once we got busy clearing the yard yesterday. Exercise does that, I guess."

"Yes, I know it's helped me to cope with the shock by walking around town handing out flyers. Occupying my mind with this task, putting together a beautiful memorial for my dear sister, has helped me a lot. And that brings me to my question." She scrunched up her face. "I hate to ask for another favor because you've already done so much, but I took home jars of Roberta's homemade strawberry jam, and I bought some whipping cream. It won't be clotted cream, but I thought I could whip up some soft, creamy butter. Would you mind terribly bringing the scones by this afternoon? I want to put them together before the memorial."

"Absolutely. I don't mind at all. We close here at two, so I can drop them off at three. In fact, I'll stay and help you put them together."

"That's really kind of you. Thanks so much. And now I'm off to pick up the microphone and speakers I rented. I thought we could sing some of her favorite songs." She tapped her head. "That's another thing I need to do—make copies of song lyrics." She paused, and her expression saddened again. "I think Roberta would like this memorial. I only hope people show up."

"I'm sure they will. You know this town—we always come together when it has to do with the community. I'll see you later."

"Thanks again." Janice walked out with an energetic step. She certainly was quick to change from one mood to another. I supposed grief was often like that—the big ups and downs.

I walked to the kitchen. Jack had finished his coffee and was getting ready to frost a walnut cake for a birthday party.

"That was Janice, Roberta's sister," I explained. "I'm helping her put butter and jam on the scones later."

Jack nodded. His mouth was pulled tight, and he looked tense about something. I couldn't figure out what could have happened in that short amount of time that would have changed his mood so drastically.

"Jack? What's going on? Was the coffee too strong?" I asked, just to lighten the mood. It worked some. His broad shoulders relaxed.

"I got a call while you were out talking to Roberta's sister." He gently placed the first cake layer onto the decorating pedestal.

"All right," I said. "Care to elaborate? Or, if it's none of my business—"

"It was Ranger Braddock. He'd like me to come in for questioning after I get off work." Jack had some history with the law, and Dalton had been firmly against me hiring him as an assistant. For that matter, I got the same grief from Cade about the hire. But the two had been very wrong and I'd been very right. Cade had admitted as much, but Dalton not so much and because of that Jack and Dalton had never grown to be friends. They were polite enough to each other, but that was as far as their relationship went—a nod hello or a thank you at the counter.

I sat down, stunned and trying to absorb the news. "First of all, I'm sorry about that, Jack. Apparently, Dalton's entire investigation is based on one napkin and Roberta's teahouse that may or may not have impacted the bakery. Just answer his questions honestly and don't worry about it. I'm going to talk to him, but most importantly, I'm going to find the real killer."

"I don't have an alibi. I was alone all day on Sunday," Jack lamented.

"I'm going to take care of this." I walked over to him. "I'm sorry, Jack."

Jack nodded and dug his rubber scraper into the bowl of frosting. "It seems Braddock has never learned to trust me." His disappointed tone broke my heart.

"That's not it, Jack. He called me in, too. He'll probably tell you a hundred times before he even asks the first question that he's just doing his job. And that's all there is to it."

Jack plopped a pile of fluffy buttercream on the cake. "How is the investigation going? Any closer to the real killer?"

"I've talked to the people with the most motive. Some facts, historical details, came up about the two sisters. It seems that Janice dated Harry before Roberta, but obviously, Roberta ended up with him. But that was years ago, and it seems like a flimsy reason to kill your sister decades later. Janice had left town after she and Harry broke up, and when she returned, her sister had married him."

"Seems like that would be the time to clobber your sister," he blurted. "Sorry, that was in bad taste."

"No, it's fine. And I agree. That's when you strike—when the coals are hot. Not decades later when all the sparks are extinguished. Gee, look at me and all my cool analogies today. Anyhow, there is some mystery about who broke up the relationship between Harry and Janice, but finding out won't get me any closer to the killer. Don't worry—Inspector Ramone is on it, and Ranger Braddock is going to feel very silly about his flimsy case."

thirty

. . .

JACK LEFT EARLY. He wanted to shower and change to look *presentable* for the questioning. It was so cute I couldn't let him leave without a big hug. I told him to wear his blue shirt because it made him look more sophisticated. He laughed and walked out. There was still plenty of tension in his beefy shoulders.

I finished cleaning up and walked to the door to lock it. As I glanced out, I spotted Mallory across the road, walking past the market. She was with someone, but I couldn't see who until Mallory paused to tie her shoe. It was Arnie. I hadn't realized they were friends. I decided it was time for some real sleuthing. I slipped out the bakery door, locked it and then started down my side of the sidewalk. The two were deep in conversation and didn't take the time to look around at all. I stayed back just far enough to keep out of their peripheral view.

They reached the end of the sidewalk, glanced back and forth casually and then crossed the road. They were heading toward the park. They continued their chat and didn't notice me, but as they reached the park, Mallory looked back, almost as if she suspected they were being followed. I ducked around the corner. Admittedly, a surge of adrenaline went through me. It was fun following a suspect. Or maybe two suspects? Both Mallory and Arnie had reason to be angry with Roberta. Perhaps they'd pooled that rage and plotted a murder.

I peeked around the corner. The pair had entered the park. They were crossing the gravel parking lot and heading toward the chess tables. Maybe they were chess partners. It was a stretch but also a slim possibility. The chess tables had their usual sets of players, mostly retired men who spent nice-weather days sitting at the tables doing more debating and arguing than playing.

My theory about them being chess partners came to an end when they made a sharp turn toward the picnic benches. I couldn't just walk up to them and ask what they were talking about. A touch of eavesdropping felt like a good move, and it went along nicely with my stealthy maneuvering down the sidewalk.

Green Lake Park was named for the tiny lake in the middle of the grounds. The emerald green color of the water came from a combination of algae and shade from the surrounding evergreens. There was a nice walking path that took you all the way around the lake. It was an easy stroll that was always enjoyable. Normally, I'd take a quick trip around for a touch of exercise and to watch the birds and squirrels. All the animals were energetic and getting ready for spring. A robin flew right past my face carrying a big chunk of grass in its beak. Nests were being built in every tree, and by summer, baby birds would be hopping around the park after their parents.

At the far end of the lake, the path forked off and adventurous types could take a second trail that had a little more to it, namely a slight uphill slope and the occasional rocky outcropping. It also led to the picnic tables. There were enough trees to use for my highly covert operation.

I walked along the trail and glanced through the trees as I moved. I passed the chess tables, which meant I was getting close to the picnic tables. If I went too far, I'd end up past the trees, and my targets would see me. I could hear their voices, but they were still just a distant mumble. It sounded like a casual, light conversation, based on the tone. I stepped over a fallen tree and snuggled behind a pair of spruce trees. They'd grown into each other, their flat branches crisscrossing and creating a nice wall of evergreen. I leaned in, and once my own breathing from the walk had slowed, I could hear them more clearly.

"I think it's a great plan. Solves both of our problems," Mallory said. I'd missed the first part of the conversation, so I had no idea what plan they were talking about, but it sounded like something that might happen in the future. Not something that had already taken place—like a murder plot.

"Who knew that this event would bring us together?" Arnie said.

Had they started a relationship? Mallory was a good twenty years older but then she did pride herself on being young and edgy. May-December romances happened all the time. The question was—exactly what was it that brought them together? Roberta's death or their shared rage that led to them killing their mutual nemesis?

I had the perfect secret location, and I could overhear their conversation. It was a win for Scottie the sleuth, but a big loss for Scottie, granddaughter of Evie. Nana would not be pleased about this, and if it hadn't been for the dejected way Jack had walked out of the bakery earlier, I probably wouldn't have done it. Jack had been trying hard to reestablish his worth in society, and Dalton calling him in for questioning had set him back. I knew Jack well now, and it would take him a few weeks to get past this.

"Are you going to the memorial tonight?" Arnie asked.

They were finally touching on the main subject. I leaned closer, not wanting to miss a word. As I glanced down at the ground, a bull snake wriggled past. It wasn't a rattler, but that didn't stop me from squeaking in alarm.

"Did you hear that?" Mallory asked. "Sounds like a squirrel is in trouble."

I pressed my fingers against my mouth to stifle a laugh. It seemed my covert operation had come to a slithery end. I straightened my posture, smoothed my hair back and stepped casually out from my hiding spot. I opened my eyes wide. "Oh, hello, I was just out for an afternoon walk. Nice day, isn't it?"

They seemed to buy my story.

"Did you step on a squirrel tail back there?" Mallory asked.

I chuckled. "A squirrel? No, that was probably me you heard. I saw a snake."

Mallory stood up in alarm and leaned over to check the ground around her feet. "I hate snakes."

"Do ya?" Arnie asked. "Well, you're in luck, then. I love 'em, and I'm great at catching and relocating them. Even the mean ones, like rattlesnakes. So, if you find one in your garden, then all you have to do is give your ole roommate a call."

Seemed I was going to have to thank a bull snake. It just

helped me get to the bottom of their new partnership. "Roommate?" I asked. "So, you found a new place to stay, Arnie?"

"Sure did. Mallory heard through the grapevine that Roberta had evicted me from the rental. We ran into each other down the hill at the gas station and started talking."

Mallory satisfied herself that the snake had not come our way. She sat down again. "I've got two spare bedrooms, and it'll be nice to have someone around to talk to and who can fix things and, gosh, catch snakes, I guess. That's a big bonus."

"Sounds like the perfect plan. Are the two of you going to the memorial tonight?" I asked.

Mallory was shaking her head no just as Arnie seemed ready to say yes. "I can't," Mallory said. "I'm just too distraught about my teapot. I'll send Harry a nice card and bake him something in a few weeks, but right now, the betrayal is too raw."

Arnie patted her hand. "I don't blame you, Mallory. I'm going to go for Harry's sake. He was always nice to me even if Roberta was a constant thorn in my side. How about you, Scottie?"

"I'll be there. I'm going to Janice's house right now to help her fill scones with butter and jam. We'll be serving them at the memorial."

"That'll be a nice touch," Arnie said. He stood up. "I've got more things to pack. I'll start bringing the stuff over tomorrow if that's all right, Mallory?"

"Yes, I'm going to spend the rest of the evening cleaning that room and spare bathroom, so it'll be ready for you." Nothing about the way they were behaving seemed untoward. They appeared genuinely pleased with their future plans. It didn't necessarily clear them of murder, but, at the same time, it didn't make them look guilty.

We all walked out of the park together, speaking only of benign topics like the weather and the geese on the lake. I waved goodbye to them and headed back to the bakery for my purse and coat. For a moment there, I thought I was onto something significant, but this encounter, like all the rest, ended with me no closer to finding Roberta's killer.

thirty-one

. . .

I'D USED bakery boxes to pack the scones. I carried the boxes up the brick path leading to Janice's door. A wreath of pink silk peonies hung on the door, celebrating the arrival of spring. Janice greeted me at the door with a melancholy smile. She was clutching a tissue as if she worried she might break into sobs any moment, but I didn't see any tears. "This is so good of you, Scottie." I handed her two of the boxes to shorten the tower I was holding. A fat orange cat hopped up and flew off the back of a plaid sofa when it saw the stranger with pink boxes. Six chairs, like the ones now sitting at Cade's kitchen table, encircled a round walnut dining table. A vase of sunflowers sat in the middle of the table. The small dining area was surrounded by antiques, including a Victorian-style buffet and a large silver tea set. The hand-carved wooden box that Janice bought back from her sister at the yard sale sat on the buffet next to the tea service. Janice had been angry when she saw the box, which had belonged to their grandmother, sitting so unceremoniously out on a yard sale table.

"I've brewed us some nice green tea, good for your health and full of antioxidants," Janice said as I followed her into the kitchen. It was a cozy room with a red and white enamel farm table and matching red chairs. Red and white checked curtains hung over the two windows on each side of the sink. We placed the boxes of scones on the end of the table where Janice had everything ready to go for a factory style scone assembly line. She'd scooped the jam from the jars into a large bowl. Freshly whipped butter was piled high in a second bowl.

"Shall we have tea first?" she asked.

"Sure."

"I forgot the table was filled. Let's drink our tea out in the dining room."

I was anxious to finish the task and get back home to check on Nana, but sipping tea would also give me an opportunity to pry a little more information out of Janice. We sat down in her dining room.

"These chairs are wonderful. Cade has his around his kitchen table, and he's very pleased with them," I said.

Janice's cheeks rolled up with a smile as she set the tea down. "I'm so glad they found a good home. Roberta had them stacked up in the garage," she said with an edge of disgust. "They're so dear to me, but Roberta treated them with little regard. This Victorian buffet used to be in the teahouse, too. Roberta knew I wanted it. At first, she tried to fight me for it, then she noticed all the tea stains on top and decided it had no market value. I told her that it was priceless in my eyes. She always saw dollar signs where I saw hearts. We were very different." Janice paused to look sad, but it looked rehearsed. I wondered if she'd been practicing in the mirror to put on a proper look of grief at the memorial.

"How is Harry doing?" I asked.

"I've been so busy with the memorial; I've hardly had time to talk to him. Poor dear is broken up about it, of course." She ended her statement with a small twist of her mouth as if she found his grief not worthy of empathy.

"I've heard that you and Harry were quite the couple in high school."

Janice's face popped up from her tea. "Oh my, where did you hear that?" She rolled her eyes. "Never mind. I know it was probably Regina. She does love to gossip."

She wasn't wrong there, but I didn't want to hold Regina responsible. "Actually, I've heard it from a few people. I suppose the shocking news of Roberta's death has people reminiscing about the past. You two were high school sweethearts?" I said it in a teasing, girl-talk sort of way, just two gals talking about boys.

Janice's usual soft-expression and kind gaze hardened. "That's just nonsense. Clearly, Harry ended up with my sister," she said sharply. "Oh, I've got a tin of butter cookies that will go perfectly with this tea." Before I could let her know I didn't need any cookies, she fled the dining room as if a wildfire was chasing her.

I glanced around at the antiques. A corner of paper was sticking out of the old box she'd bought from Roberta. I got up to take a closer look at the carving. Roses and ivy vines had been intricately carved into the mahogany wood. I opened the box to push the paper back inside. My gaze caught the first words. They were written with black ink in stylish printing, very curly and feminine, as if it was going to be a romantic letter.

Dearest Harry,

I'm sorry, but this is no longer going to work. I don't love you. I don't want to marry you. Please don't take this too hard. I'm sure you'll find someone else soon.

Sincerely,
Janice

I glanced behind me. I could hear Janice rummaging through cupboards looking for the tin of cookies. I wasn't sure what all of it meant, but my intuition told me I was looking at a key piece of evidence. Footsteps alerted me to Janice's return. I jammed the note back into the box and gently shut the lid.

I hadn't returned to my seat yet, and Janice looked at me with a suspicious tilt of her head. I smoothed my hand over the top of the buffet. "I think the tea stains add character to it."

That comment erased the suspicion. "I agree." She set the tin of butter cookies on the table.

We sat down again to finish our tea. I felt somewhat guilty about nosing around, but there was just enough contradiction surrounding Janice and Harry's past relationship to make the note seem important. It now seemed certain that Janice was the one to break it off with Harry.

"I suppose you're feeling at ease now knowing that there won't be any teahouse to hurt your business."

I tried not to show my surprise. I had no idea Janice knew anything about the very light tension between Roberta and me over her new business. Apparently, she'd figured that out on her own.

"I wouldn't have minded having a teahouse in town. My

bakery might have lost a bit of business from it, but I would much rather have a teahouse than your sister's murder." My words were just sharp enough to make her flinch.

"Yes, of course. Naturally," she said and pried open the tin. "Cookie?"

"No, thank you. The tea is fine. Is everything ready for the memorial?" It was time for a less touchy subject. "How many people do you expect?"

"Everything is ready to go. I'm not sure how many people will show up." I was sure I caught a hint of an amused grin as if she didn't think it would be many. She definitely wasn't a sister mired in grief but then it was now solid in my mind that the two sisters weren't the least bit close.

She snapped the lid shut on the cookie tin. "Well, shall we put the scones together? I've got everything ready, and I don't want the butter to sit too long."

"Absolutely. Just tell me what to do." I noticed a corner of the note was still sticking out of the box. I was sure I was onto something. I just wasn't sure what. If she broke it off with Harry, Janice had no reason to despise her sister for marrying him. She willingly walked away from their relationship. And the whole thing happened so long ago. Why would Janice wait until now to take out her revenge on her sister? And why only Roberta? Why not take Harry out, too? It was such a flimsy motive; I had to push it aside for now. Maybe the memorial would help trigger a new line of investigation.

thirty-two

. . .

JANICE HAD HUNG clusters of pearl white balloons from the trees in Harry's yard. There were a few electric candles flickering on a podium with a microphone, and several of the mourners had brought flower bouquets, but since there hadn't been any thought given to vases and water, the bouquets were piled on the ground in front of the podium. All in all, it was a decent turnout. I'd expected it. Whether you were well-loved or not, the Ripple Creek community mourned anyone's passing. And speaking of well-loved ... Nana put on her dark gray skirt and a matching shawl for the memorial. She'd been out of action for the last few days and hadn't made any trips into town, so, naturally, her arrival matched that of a famous pop star. Everyone rushed to get the latest update and give concerned advice about how best to recuperate from a broken wrist. I left her with her adoring fans and walked up to the tables where Janice was setting the prepared scones on napkins. She mumbled fretfully as I reached her.

"What's wrong? Anything I can do?" I asked.

"Just look, Scottie. The butter is dripping out the sides. It's much warmer tonight than I expected." She busily tried to wipe up some drips of butter off the table with a handful of napkins.

I placed my hand on her arm. "No one will mind a little drip of butter. Why don't you go talk to the mourners? I'm sure everyone has offers of condolences waiting." I glanced around. "Where's Harry?"

Janice stopped blotting up the butter and looked around. "I'll go find him. Scottie, let people know they can eat the scones now—before they slide away on a river of melted butter."

"I'll let them know."

Janice hurried toward the house to find Harry.

I used my biggest voice. "Everyone, we've made scones with butter and jam. Please help yourself."

The crowd slowly made their way to the scones. I slipped past them. Dalton had just arrived and was making his way across the lawn. I reached him. "Scones with butter and jam, but a little messy. Might put grease stains on your uniform." I said it just harshly enough to grab his attention.

He looked at me. That gaze of his was always disarming, even now when we were about to get into one of our scuffles. "I had to cross Jack off my list. I'm just doing my—"

I held up my hand. "I swear, Dalton, if you tell me that one more time, I'm going to make you eat one of those scones ... without a napkin." My quip helped ease the tension before it really got started.

"Jack didn't kill Roberta," I said.

"I know that."

"I wish you had crossed his name off without actually questioning him, because you know how hurt he gets when he thinks people don't trust him."

"He'll be fine. He's a grown man."

I rolled my eyes. We both scanned the crowd. "Do you think the killer will return to the scene of the crime?" I asked.

"He's already here." Dalton nodded his head in the direction of the podium area. Arnie was dropping a bouquet of flowers on the pile.

"Arnie? Surely not. I spoke to him several times, and …" I let my words trail off when I was on the receiving end of a lifted brow. "Well, I'll just let you get on with your investigation."

"Thank you," he said wryly. "Arnie has motive. Roberta was trying to unfairly evict him from the house he'd been renting from her for years."

"Yes, but he was already packing up to leave. In fact, he's going to rent a room from Mallory." That detail caught his attention. I shrugged cockily. "Guess that's news to you. In your defense, I think they only just decided on it. And you do know that Harry was high school sweethearts with Janice, Roberta's sister, before things went awry and Harry married Roberta."

"I've interviewed both Harry and Janice, and I found no reason to suspect either of them. Their relationship was in high school, and we both know that school crushes don't hold water after many years." He said it so pointedly, I could almost see punctuation in the air around the words.

"Other than a possible motive, what evidence do you have connecting Arnie to the crime?" I asked.

"He admitted he was here, at the house, on Sunday morning."

I laughed. "Hardly convincing."

"I'm going to grab one of those messy scones. They're very tasty." He was countering my abrasiveness with his own.

"You do realize Roberta didn't bake those, right?" I called to his back.

He turned around and looked at me from under derisive brows. "I assumed that was the case."

"Just making sure since you seem so fond of her scones. I wonder who did bake them?" I asked and then grinned smugly at him.

"Maybe I'll skip the scone," he said and headed in Arnie's direction. I was almost a hundred percent certain he was focused on the wrong suspect.

My gaze happened to float across the yard toward the house where I spotted Janice hurrying after Harry. He was stomping toward the back of the garage, and they both looked upset. It was time to put back on my super sleuthing hat and do some eavesdropping. Of course, I would never consider it if they weren't now my two prime suspects. Obviously, eavesdropping was wrong, but when it came to murder, all etiquette was off the table.

I could hear Harry speaking sharply as I scooted quietly along the side of the garage. "No, Janice, that just can't be. I don't believe you. She'd never do that."

"Harry, my love, don't you see? We were meant to be together. The two of us would have been married if not for her."

A deep voice cleared behind me, startling me from my semi-crouch. I spun around. Dalton crossed his arms and gave me an annoying fatherly scowl. But that didn't matter. I'd come across something big … maybe.

I sensed that the conversation around the corner was coming to an end when I heard Harry say, "Leave me alone, Janice."

I grabbed Dalton's hand and pulled him back toward the yard but then made a sharp right toward the house. I wanted to talk to him without all the townsfolk milling about, eating buttery scones. My eyes scanned the yard to make sure no one was within hearing distance. That was when I noticed one mourner in particular. Cade had mentioned possibly dropping by, but I hadn't expected him. He was staring straight at us, and from the expression he wore, he'd just witnessed me leading Dalton, by the hand, no less, to a secluded part of the front yard. My stomach dropped to my feet. I pushed up a smile and waved at him.

He responded with a very male chin lift. This was going to take some explaining and probably a lot of groveling. Harry came shuffling around the corner with a grimace on his face, reminding me I had something important to get to first.

My enthusiasm for solving the case had just taken a big hit, but I had to forge ahead. I sensed that I was getting closer to solving it. "Look, I think something is going on between Janice and Harry. Maybe those old flames haven't died yet. I don't know how it's all connected, and I haven't figured out a motive yet but—"

"But? That's a big but." He chuckled at his phrasing. "Why don't you leave the investigation to me, Scottie? I think Arnie is the killer."

"And I think you're wrong," I said, emphatically.

"Care to make a wager on it?" he asked, teasingly.

There was no way to deny the whole thing had become a little flirtatious. That realization felt like a cold shower. I straightened. "No, let's just see what happens," I said, my posture straight and serious.

"No, let's not see. You stay out of it, and let me do my—" He paused. "You know what I mean." He turned to leave. "Oh look, Rafferty's here." There was no attempt to hide his annoyance. "Hmm, and there's Tanya. Remember what I said. Stay out of it." Admittedly there wasn't much conviction in his command because he knew too well that I was going to ignore it.

I took a deep breath and headed across to where Cade had been cornered by a few locals who were also his fans. He spotted me, made excuses and strolled toward me.

"Did you have a nice chat with Braddock?"

"We were talking about the case," I said. "I'm still working on finding the killer, and he's heading in the wrong direction."

"Not surprising. He's an Inspector Gadget without any actual gadgets."

"Dalton is not a cartoon detective, but he's still wrong, this time."

"And you need to hold hands with him to get that point across?" Cade's hazel gaze locked with mine.

"I was pulling him away from the garage, so Harry didn't catch me eavesdropping on his conversation with Janice. There's something going on between them, and I think it's the key to solving the case." I took his hand. "See, this, this is me holding the hand of the man I love. That—what you saw earlier—was nothing of the sort."

Cade nodded and squeezed my hand in his. He looked at the balloons hanging from the trees. Music, an upbeat country song, started playing through the speakers. "I'm confused. Are we mourning the woman or celebrating her untimely demise?"

"I'm not exactly sure, but I don't think Janice is too broken up about her sister's death. And I'm holding onto that because I think I've just figured something out."

Cade's smile had a nice hint of admiration. "That's my clever little detective."

thirty-three
. . .

NANA WAS EXHAUSTED from all the attention. It was a memorial to pay tribute to Roberta Schubert, and it was nice with people nibbling scones and singing the songs that Roberta loved, but only a few people spoke about Roberta. Harry was such a shattered mess, he couldn't say much more than "Roberta was a good wife, and she made the best fried chicken and mashed potatoes." Janice didn't say anything, but she made sure everyone knew she'd organized the event, and she led the singing. I saw her try and approach Harry several times, but he was always surrounded by neighbors and friends. It seemed almost as if he was using them as a shield to avoid talking to Janice.

Nana pulled her shawl closer around her as we got out of the car. "It's getting nippy out. I should take some soup over to Hannah." Hannah had stayed home with a sore throat.

"I'll take it to her. The last thing you need is a sore throat and cold, Nana. One catastrophe at a time. And if you go, Hannah will want you to stay and tell her all the gossip."

Nana's chuckle was hoarse. She'd done so much talking at the memorial, she'd have a sore throat anyway. "You're so right about that, and I've got a whole catalogue of topics to discuss. Boy, you lock yourself away for a short week, and the whole town comes apart at the seams." We walked inside. It was much cozier inside the cottage than out in the front yard. Spring was in the air, but when the sun dropped you could still feel winter blowing through the trees.

"I can make you a grilled cheese sandwich to eat with a cup of leftover lentil soup."

"Oh yes, that would be wonderful." I helped her take off her shawl. She walked to the couch and immediately covered her knees with the throw blanket. "You know, I'm getting rather used to this pampered lifestyle."

"Well, I've enjoyed getting to be the pamperer for a change. However, I'm also anxious to see you back to a hundred percent." I walked into the kitchen.

"Button, pull out the container of chicken noodle soup from the freezer." Nana always had a batch of homemade chicken noodle soup in the freezer for colds and flus. "Are you sure you don't want me to walk it over to Hannah? The last thing you need is a cold with your busy work schedule. Plus, who'll pamper me if you're sick in bed?" She laughed at her comment.

"I'm just going to hand it to her and let her know to call if she needs us." Roberta's handwritten recipe card was sitting where I'd left it on the kitchen counter. I'd come up with an interesting theory while standing at the memorial, and I was hoping the recipe card would move that theory along. I picked up the card and a shot of adrenaline went through me. Curly letters. Roberta wrote in a very flowery, almost artsy script. I remembered thinking how contradictory the style seemed for Roberta, a woman who prided herself on being stern and pragmatic. The letter that really caught my eye was the letter "S" in "Mother's Scones." Roberta added a curlicue at the top and bottom of the letter. The *Dear John* or, more accurately, *Dear Harry* letter in the antique box was written in similar script, and the capital "S" in "Sincerely" had the same curly flourishes at the top and bottom. I noticed it because in junior high I'd tried to spruce up my handwriting by adding in cutesy curls. I wanted to develop my own style. My English teacher was not a fan. My first essay in my fancy, new script was crisscrossed with angry red marks, and on the side, she noted that she couldn't read half the words. That was the end of my fancy handwriting debut.

I pushed aside the card for now. I would need to see a sample of Janice's writing, and I had no idea how to go about that. But for now, my theory was holding.

I pulled out the ingredients for grilled cheese and took the container of chicken soup out of the freezer.

"Button, could I get a glass of orange juice? I'm worn out from standing and talking to everyone for so long."

"Absolutely." I was trying to ignore the fact that this injury had somehow made Nana suddenly seem much older. I was sure she'd get back to her old self soon enough, but this past week had really caused me to start grappling with the reality that I might someday be without her, and that thought was incredibly overwhelming. I poured myself a glass, too. I needed it.

I carried the two glasses out to the front room and sat with her to enjoy the juice.

Nana sipped some juice and released a satisfied sigh. "I don't understand how one broken wrist can cause me to lose all my stamina."

"It was a long afternoon."

"It sure was, and I must say, there was one main theme throughout the whole memorial."

I sat up straighter. "Really? What was that?"

Nana noticed she had my full, undivided attention. She took another sip to draw out the drama. She smiled. "Hmm, that is delicious."

"Nana," I pleaded.

"All right. I'm just teasing. Everyone noticed how Janice wasn't the least bit sad or upset or grief-stricken. I know the two sisters weren't close, but she didn't show a lick of emotion when she talked about her sister or when she introduced her favorite songs. Nothing. It was as if she was the emcee at an event that had no real connection to her life."

"I agree. I've seen very little emotion from Roberta's sister, and I can add that to my newest theory."

Now I had Nana's undivided attention, but my grandmother had an uncanny ability to read my mind. "You think Janice killed Roberta?"

"That's the theory I'm working on. I'm going to deliver the soup and then I'll get started on your sandwich. I'll let Hannah know you've got a whole catalogue of topics for your next visit."

thirty-four

. . .

JACK WAS STILL in a funk about being called into the station. We were mostly silent as we baked breads, pastries and cookies for the day. "If it helps at all," I said as we started to carry the treats to the front of the shop, "I spoke to Dalton, and he doesn't think you're the killer."

"Good of him—considering I'm *not* the killer," he said curtly and returned to the kitchen. I knew Jack. He'd work through the anger soon. A busy day at the bakery would do the trick.

In the meantime, I was trying to figure out the best way to prove my theory. Nothing came to me during our busy morning, but I was sure I'd think of something. Up until now, Janice hadn't made a good suspect. She didn't really have a strong motive to kill her sister, other than the fact that they weren't great friends. Roberta had married Harry years before, so if that had been her motive it seemed she'd have confronted her sister long ago. But if my theory held, I'd found a spectacular motive. I had also started to pull on other threads. One of the bakery napkins had been found at the scene, which made me wonder if the killer was trying to frame me. Janice mentioned to me that I was probably relieved there'd be no teahouse. At the time I'd assured her that wasn't the case, but I wondered if she was trying to get me to admit it, so she could take my answer to Ranger Braddock as proof of motive. It was a wild stretch, but it kept poking around in the back of my mind.

"I'm turning the sign!" I called to the back. It was what we said whenever one of us was about to flip the sign to open. I turned it over, lifted my face and gasped. A face was staring back at me. I laughed. It was Cade. He pulled open the door.

"I thought it would be a sexy move, standing here, watching you turn the sign, but it seems it went from sexy to creepy very quickly. I noticed a gasp."

"It wasn't really a gasp," I said, then tilted my head side to side. "All right, it was a gasp. I wasn't expecting a face to be staring in at me as I looked up."

"Duly noted. I will not try that particular move again in an attempt at being spontaneous and sexy. However, this move always seems to do the trick." He glanced around to make sure we were alone, wrapped his arm around my back and pulled me closer for a kiss. "Better?"

"Much less creepy."

"Good to know."

We walked to the counter. "You don't usually come in this early. What's up?"

"I've got a video chat with my editor in an hour, and I need a major shot of sugar. He's going to be expecting updates and first chapters, and I'm woefully behind on both." Cade was constantly fretting about deadlines, but this time I sensed he was extra uptight about it.

Bad to the Scone

I walked behind the counter. "Well, you've come to the right place for that shot of sugar." I already knew his order—a raspberry Danish and a banana muffin. The muffin was for his coffee break, but the Danish would give him that burst of energy he was hoping for. I handed him the treats. "You're really struggling, aren't you?"

Cade nodded weakly. "I've hit walls like this before, but not for this long. I'll get past it. How's the case going? Have you solved it yet?" Cade was always good at avoiding talking about a sore subject—like his writer's block—but then this probably wasn't the time or place to dive into it. It wasn't the time or place to discuss murder either, but he was the only customer at the moment.

"I think it was the sister," I said in my most clandestine tone. "And if I'm right about the motive—well—no one deserves murder, but Roberta really had it coming."

"That sounds intriguing. You'll have to tell me all about it over dinner tonight." He took a bite of Danish. "Superb. Let's hope this does the trick." He stopped on his way to the door. "Is Roberta's sister the woman who stayed glued to the microphone for the whole singalong? By the way, if I should go first, I definitely want a singalong at my memorial. Way more fun than standing around with glum expressions eating store-bought coffee cake."

"I agree. And yes, that was Janice, the victim's sister and with any luck, the killer."

"I thought so. I just saw her going into the market across the street."

"Did you? Oh wow, maybe I need a bottle of vanilla this morning. Thanks for the tip."

"Sure thing, but try not to antagonize the murderess. You know that sometimes ends badly. Thanks for the pastries."

"See you later. And take a walk around your property. You know that always helps you get ideas."

"Good suggestion." He walked out.

I untied my apron. "Jack," I said with a sympathetic smile.

"I heard. Go on then. I'll watch the front of the shop."

"Thanks."

"And find the killer, would ya?"

"I plan to do just that," I said. "Just not sure how," I muttered to myself. I passed several customers who were walking in. They looked at me in confusion. "Jack will help ya. I'll be right back."

I couldn't believe my luck when I stepped into the market. Janice was standing in the produce area, and she was checking off items on a grocery list—a handwritten grocery list.

"Morning, Scottie." Tanya waved energetically from behind the checkout counter. "Roxi's in the storage room. She should be out soon."

I waved back. "Thanks."

Janice looked up over the basket of potatoes. "Scottie, how nice to see you." She waved her list lightly. I tried to glance at it, but she was holding it tightly in her fist. "I'm going to make Harry a few casseroles and put them in the freezer, so he can heat them when he wants. I feel so bad for the man. I don't think he's eaten a decent meal since—" Her face dropped dramatically, and she took a deep, solemn breath. "Well, you know."

"That's nice of you. I'm sure he'll appreciate it." I just needed a solid look at that list. I walked over to the sweet potatoes that were piled high in a mound next to the potatoes. I plucked out a large one from the bottom and immediately started an avalanche of potatoes. "Oops!" I said and frantically grabbed at the runaway potatoes.

Janice laughed and instinctively did the same. The list fell from her hand. The two of us collected up the potatoes.

A throat cleared behind me. It was Roxi. "All right, who took a sweet potato from the bottom of the heap?"

I raised my hand meekly. She had no idea that it was all part of my ploy to see Janice's list. I swept the fallen paper up from the floor and looked at it. The printing was neat and concise and not the least bit frilly. No curlicues in sight. "Thanks for your help. Your list." I handed it back to Janice.

"Thank you so much." Janice returned to her shopping.

My heart was thumping hard in my chest. I had my killer, and my theory was right. Of course, a straight-out confession would really seal the deal.

I turned back toward Janice. "It was Roberta, wasn't it? She was the one who broke you and Harry up. All those years ago she started a terrible scheme to break the two of you up—you and Harry—the man you were going to marry."

Janice blinked nervously at me. "I have no idea what you're talking about." The nervous twitch in her cheek told me she knew exactly what I was talking about.

"I saw the note. I confess I was snooping. It wasn't really snooping, but I noticed a corner of paper sticking out of the wooden box, the one you bought from Roberta. It had belonged to your grandmother and then Roberta had it until she set it out at the yard sale. Only she forgot to clear out the contents. The letter that you supposedly wrote to Harry letting him know you didn't want to get married and that the relationship was over was still in that box. You saw it—for the first time—I assume—when you purchased that box. And you knew the second you looked at it that you didn't write the letter. It was Roberta's handwriting. I know that because Harry gave me Roberta's recipe card for scones. The curlicues, the frilly letters, that's Roberta's writing."

Roxi and Tanya had tuned in now, realizing there was a heavy conversation taking place in their produce department. It would be good to have witnesses for the confession.

"Roberta wrote you a letter, too, only it was from Harry. He was breaking up with you."

"I should have known. The writing was all wrong. She tried to hide her own writing and used hard, sharp strokes. At the time, I assumed Harry was upset as he wrote it. We never talked about it. We were both so hurt, we couldn't face one another, and all that time Roberta, my own sister, had contrived the entire diabolical plan." Her voice grew shaky and her face red. "We were in love! I saw that note in the box and knew immediately that Roberta had written it. She always won penmanship awards for that clownish scribble."

"How? How did you manage it?"

Now that the floodgates were open, Janice seemed glad to let the confession flow. "I had no plans to kill her, but she was so awful, so cruel about it. I showed up at the yard sale. She was alone. I started picking up anything that had belonged to my mom or grandmother. I told her I was taking it all home, and she couldn't stop me. She raced over and tried to fight me for it. We struggled for a second and then I stopped and stared at her—hard. I told her that I knew what she'd done, that she'd written notes to break up Harry and me. I told her I was going to let Harry know and that the two of us were going to get back together." She scoffed. "Turns out Harry's been so henpecked all these years; he's lost all his courage. He wouldn't believe me, even when I showed him the note. He said I was trying to ruin his memory of Roberta."

She'd strayed from her confession. I needed to turn her back toward it.

"How did it happen? The murder?" I asked.

"Roberta pushed me. She told me I wasn't allowed to speak to Harry ever again. I pushed her back. She fell on her bottom. I lunged at her, but she got up and ran right through the plants to her neighbor's yard. She raced through the back gate, but I caught up to her. I shoved her, and she flew forward. She was terrified." Janice laughed. It had an evil edge to it. "Her eyes bulged with fear. She pushed to a half crawl and ran into the shed. There was a piece of rope hanging in the lock. Oscar must have been using it to hold the shed door shut. I pulled the rope free and yanked the door right out of her grasp. It's amazing how strong you grow when you're fueled by rage. She, on the other hand, trembled with fear. I caught her easily." I could hear Tanya and Roxi suck in quiet gasps.

"Did you put the bakery napkin next to her body to frame me?"

Janice shrugged nonchalantly as if we were just discussing the weather and not her murder scheme. "I'd seen you at the yard sale the day before, and I knew that Roberta had been bragging about how her new business was going to take away from the bakery business. The napkin was sticking out of Roberta's pocket when I—" Suddenly, after her very detailed description, it seemed to dawn on her that she'd just confessed to murder.

I wasn't ready for what happened next. Janice shoved me hard, so hard that I fell on my bottom. She hurried past me to make her escape.

thirty-five
. . .

ROXI AND TANYA rushed over to help me up. I'd landed painfully on my tailbone. I rubbed my bottom as I got to my feet. "We need to call Dalton," I said.

"For what?" Dalton walked in right then.

Roxi raced over to him. "Did you see Janice?"

"She just raced past me," Dalton said.

"Yes, she was in a bit of a hurry," I explained, still rubbing my bottom. "She just confessed to murdering Roberta."

Dalton stared at me a second as if he didn't believe me.

"She did," Roxi said urgently. "Tanya and I heard every word. She killed her sister." Roxi looked at me. "I'm still a little fuzzy about why she did it."

"I'll explain later. We've got to catch her." I grabbed Dalton's hand and then quickly released it. (I really needed to stop doing that.)

Dalton and I hurried out to the sidewalk. "She must have driven off," I said. "We need to go after her."

"We?" he asked wryly.

I stared up at him. "Seriously? I find the killer, get a fabulously detailed confession out of her and I sustain a bruise to my tailbone in the process, and you're not going to let me be part of the high-speed chase?"

"We're in a small mountain town. I doubt any high-speed chase is in the future." I took that as his decision to let me tag along.

I followed him to the truck. "Don't you have a bakery to run?"

"Oops, right. I'll let Jack know I'm out to catch a criminal and then I'll be back." I glanced across to the bakery and saw only two heads through the window. It was a slow morning again. I supposed I couldn't blame it on Roberta's scones this time. Maybe people were just taking a break from the sweets and fresh breads, or maybe it was time to create some new treats.

We climbed into the truck. "I guess I'll drive toward her house," Dalton said. "In the meantime—what was her motive?"

"First of all, she was trying to frame me. She knew Roberta was bragging about putting a dent in my business, and my bakery napkin was conveniently tucked in Roberta's pocket so she pulled it free and dropped it in the shed. And it seems her plan worked." I smiled smugly at Dalton.

"I'm never going to live that down, am I?"

"Not for a very long time."

"Why did Janice kill Roberta? Did it have to do with Harry?" He looked at me. "Was Harry involved?"

"He was the reason behind the motive, but he wasn't involved. In fact, when I saw him at the memorial, something tells me he was starting to think that Janice was the killer. He wanted nothing to do with her. Janice found a note, the one that she'd supposedly written to Harry, way back when they were a couple. It said that she was breaking it off with him."

"Let me guess—Roberta actually wrote the note?"

I nodded. "Yep. Roberta sent the same kind of letter to her sister signed by Harry. She orchestrated the whole thing to break them up, then she swooped in and married Harry. All these years, Janice believed that Harry had just fallen out of love with her, and he thought the same about her. It was a cruel plan. Roberta did something awful, but I'm not sure she deserved to die."

Dalton pointed ahead. "Looks like she didn't make it home."

Janice's car was parked on the side of the road. She was leaned against the back of it sobbing into her hands. We stopped and got out of the truck.

Janice lifted her hands showing she was ready to be cuffed. "Ranger Braddock, I've done something horrible. I killed my sister. Please take me in, lock me up and throw away the key."

thirty-six
. . .

AFTER THE ADVENTURE-FILLED MORNING, I returned to the bakery and narrated the whole story to Jack. Business picked up enough that we ended up having a good day. We did, however, talk about adding some new delights to our spring and summer menus. We just hadn't decided what yet.

Hannah's sore throat miraculously disappeared. She gave credit to Nana's magical noodle soup. I left them sitting on the couch while Hannah listened raptly to all the gossip Nana heard at the memorial. I got dressed and drove over to Cade's house. He'd texted that the writer's block had been broken, and he claimed to have a good but humiliating story to go with it.

The days were getting longer, and soon, we'd have daylight well into the evening. The sun was just starting to tuck itself behind one of the western peaks, so the big house was bathed in shadowy dusk. For years, it was abandoned and overgrown with weeds and vines, so naturally, it became the haunted house of the neighborhood. My friends and I used to ride our bikes up to the house and dare each other to look through dusty windows. We always managed to leave there shrieking in fear and bursting with adrenaline. We'd race our bikes back down the gravel drive and promise never to visit the creepy old house again. We never held to that promise, but it always seemed like the logical agreement to make after being scared witless by the place.

My breath caught in my chest as my extremely handsome boyfriend opened the front door. His longish hair was brushed back off his face, and he was wearing a light blue shirt that highlighted his complexion. I picked up my pace and hurried into his embrace. A nice, sweet kiss followed and then we went inside.

"So, once again, Scottie Ramone has brought justice to Gotham City."

I laughed. "Well, Gotham City might be an overreach; however, we do have our share of villains. Janice confessed the whole thing to me as we stood in the produce section of the market. Roxi and Tanya witnessed the whole thing, so I'd say Dalton's case against her is rock solid."

Cade scoffed. "He needs all the help he can get."

I squeezed Cade's arm. "Let's skip that topic, tonight, eh? It's a beautiful spring night, and you have your favorite baker by your side. We'll push murder out of our heads and concentrate on the evening ahead."

We walked into his sitting room, and I plopped down on my favorite sofa. "You mentioned the writer's block is gone?"

Cade sat down next to me. He had a bottle of wine and some cheese and crackers already sitting on the coffee table in front of us. "It is and I suppose, in a roundabout way, I have you to thank for that."

"Really? Way to go, me. I'm really on a roll today. What happened?"

"Now, I'll tell you, but please, don't laugh. I already chastised myself enough for it, and frankly, the humiliation was so great I couldn't even face the squirrels that were hanging out in the garden."

"Sounds extremely serious." A statement I contradicted with a grin.

"Maybe I shouldn't tell you. You're already in smirk mode."

I took hold of his arm. "No, please, I promise I'll be very mature about it. No more smirks. No giggles." I pulled down a fake shade in front of my face to show that I was ready to listen.

"Fine. As usual, the words were coming in slow, plodding chunks. Wait, did I tell you my new concept? I scrapped my first two, and my editor loves this new idea."

I sat up, interested. "It seems you've been keeping a great deal from me, Mr. Rafferty What's the new concept?"

"A man wakes up from a coma and is convinced that he is the infamous Dr. Frankenstein. Hilarity ensues," he said, then laughed. "No, not really."

"Yes, I figured you were kidding, considering you write gothic thrillers. Sounds great. Is the new concept what helped relieve the writer's block?"

"Well, it was the first chink in the wall. I walked out to the garden to water the plants, and as I stepped around to the hose spigot, I spotted something that looked like a snake. I jumped back, and my heart jumped, too."

"Was it a bull snake?" I asked.

"Nope."

My eyes widened. "A rattlesnake?"

"Nope."

"A garter snake?" I asked, trying to hold back a smile.

He caught it. "Aha, I believe there was a promise made about no giggles."

"Promise will be kept." I put back on a stern expression.

"It was the garden hose."

A laugh burst from my mouth, and I quickly tried to smother it with my hand. "Sorry," I muttered between my fingers.

"It's fine. My humiliation is now complete."

"Seriously, though. I've done that before. They should make those hoses bright pink or purple. But how did that end your writer's block?"

Cade shrugged and reached for the two glasses of wine. He handed me one. "The adrenaline—something about having the wits scared out of me put me in a creative mood. I walked right inside, my heart pounding, sat down and hammered out the first two chapters on my keyboard. And I think they're pretty good. I owe it all to you for reminding me that I'm surrounded by snakes out here in the wilderness."

"Well, you're welcome." We lifted our glasses. "Here's to solving murders, smashing writer's block and avoiding snakes."

We tapped glasses and sipped our wine.

about the author

London Lovett is author of the Port Danby, Starfire, Scottie Ramone Firefly Junction and Frostfall Island Cozy Mystery series. Her cozy, clean romance series Whisper Cove Sweet Romance is also a reader favorite!

Learn more at:
www.londonlovett.com

Printed in Great Britain
by Amazon